W9-BFG-503

Sarah knew Colt was going to kiss her, and she knew she was going to be undone. . . .

His arm came around her waist, indomitable. His fingers caressed her cheek, feathering across her skin with a gentleness at odds with the strength of his hand.

"Colt . . . no." The words barely made it out of her mouth; their lack of conviction almost made them silent.

He kissed her anyway, his mouth brushing over hers, enough to start the heat inside. She didn't move—she couldn't—and a second later he kissed her again, tightening his arm around her in an act of possession. His lips claimed her, marked her as his, and she trembled inside.

He wanted her. He was going to take her, all the way. She clung to him, her hands pressed to his chest, feeling his muscles give with every move he made. No one felt like Colton Haines. No one had ever felt as good. . . .

WHAT ARE *LOVESWEPT* ROMANCES?

They are stories of true romance and touching emotion. We believe those two very important ingredients are constants in our highly sensual and very believable stories in the *LOVESWEPT* line. Our goal is to give you, the reader, stories of consistently high quality that may sometimes make you laugh, sometimes make you cry, but are always fresh and creative and contain many delightful surprises within their pages.

Most romance fans read an enormous number of books. Those they truly love, they keep. Others may be traded with friends and soon forgotten. We hope that each *LOVESWEPT* romance will be a treasure—a "keeper." We will always try to publish

LOVE STORIES YOU'LL NEVER FORGET
BY AUTHORS YOU'LL ALWAYS REMEMBER

The Editors

Loveswept® 577

Glenna McReynolds
Shameless

BANTAM BOOKS
NEW YORK · TORONTO · LONDON · SYDNEY · AUCKLAND

SHAMELESS

A Bantam Book / November 1992

LOVESWEPT® and the wave design are registered
trademarks of Bantam Books, a division of
Bantam Doubleday Dell Publishing Group, Inc.
Registered in U.S. Patent
and Trademark Office and elsewhere.

All rights reserved.
Copyright © 1992 by Glenna McReynolds.
Cover art copyright © 1992 by Joel Malmed.
No part of this book may be reproduced or transmitted
in any form or by any means, electronic or mechanical,
including photocopying, recording, or by any
information storage and retrieval system, without
permission in writing from the publisher.
For information address: Bantam Books.

If you purchased this book without a cover you should be
aware that this book is stolen property. It was reported as
"unsold and destroyed" to the publisher and neither the
author nor the publisher has received any payment for this
"stripped book."

If you would be interested in receiving protective vinyl
covers for your Loveswept books, please write to this address
for information:

Loveswept
Bantam Books
P.O. Box 985
Hicksville, NY 11802

ISBN 0-553-44140-X

Published simultaneously in the United States and Canada

Bantam Books are published by Bantam Books, a division of
Bantam Doubleday Dell Publishing Group, Inc. Its trademark,
consisting of the words "Bantam Books" and the portrayal of
a rooster, is Registered in U.S. Patent and Trademark Office
and in other countries. Marca Registrada. Bantam Books, 666
Fifth Avenue, New York, New York 10103.

PRINTED IN THE UNITED STATES OF AMERICA

OPM   0 9 8 7 6 5 4 3 2 1

To my sister, Sandy—
for believing the best is yet to come

One

The brick wall was hot against Colton Haines's back, seared by a Wyoming summer sun and burning through his shirt. It was support, though, hard and reliable, a place to get what he couldn't find elsewhere.

A mist of fine dust kicked up at the end of the alley and sheeted by him in its journey east, blown by a ceaseless wind. He swiped at a tear with the back of his hand, hating the weakness in himself even more than he hated the tears' cause. The dampness mixed with the sandy grit on his knuckles, making a patch of salty mud he wiped off on his jeans.

He couldn't stand in the alley, leaning against the back wall of Atlas Drugs, and cry. He couldn't. He'd driven the ten miles into town to get to *her.*

Sarah.

His chest constricted on a sudden breath, and he squeezed his eyes shut to hold back another tear. She had never betrayed him, not from the very beginning, not like his mother, who'd just betrayed everything.

He needed Sarah's loyalty like a lifeline. In return she deserved a man, not a twenty-year-old boy crying because his mother was—He didn't know what to call it, not even in the privacy of his own mind. "Taking a caller" was the best he could do, and even that hurt. He couldn't think about it, no more than he could stand there and cry about it.

He pushed off the wall, propelled by his anger, and walked over to use the water spigot. As he crouched next to the running stream of cool water, his glance raked the endless expanse of prairie surrounding the town of Rock Creek. A herd of antelope grazed less than a hundred yards away from the main street, proof of the town's lack of worth. His mouth tightened. Rock Creek didn't even have enough civilization to hold back a herd of skittish wild animals.

And he'd thought it was the neatest damn place on earth. He made a short sound of disgust and rose to his feet.

Cleaner, with no revealing tracks staining his cheeks, he used his wet hands to slick his hair back under his cowboy hat. He settled the brim low on his forehead and with a quick motion rubbed the dirt off his boot tops on the backs of his jeans. He didn't want to look even one tenth of one percent as torn-up as he felt. What he wanted was Sarah and the way she believed in him.

Sarah thought he was strong, and next to her he was. It was one of the many pleasures of kissing her and holding her, how he had to temper his strength so as not to scare her, or ever hurt her.

Her love and trust gave him the desire to be good, to be the best.

Sarah.

He squared his shoulders and looked out on the sea of sun-cured grass floating to the horizon, broken by coulees and occasional scrub. There was nothing for him in Rock Creek. He'd known it that day so many years ago when he and his mom had washed up in this backwater, nowhere place on a flood of grief, both broken from the loss of her husband, his father. He shouldn't have forgotten. He shouldn't have invested so much of himself in the two-bit town, so many of his dreams.

There was nothing in Rock Creek, he silently repeated, never had been, nothing except Sarah. He turned his back on the prairie and headed for the main street, the cool interior of Atlas Drugs, and the soothing comfort of the girl he loved.

Sarah knew the instant Colt stepped into the store. The bell over the door didn't jingle any differently for him, but the air changed. The weatherman could talk all he wanted about increases in atmospheric pressure; Sarah felt it every time Colton Haines walked into a room.

She turned and their eyes met briefly over the postcard rack at the front of the store. She checked where her Uncle Tobias was helping Doris Childress at the pharmacy and hoped the preacher's wife would keep him busy. She knew her uncle felt bound and beholden to report on her to her father—it was that or catch hell—and lately the comings and goings of Colt had been the priority news on any given day of the week.

Colt stayed up by the tourist goods, where the display of T-shirts hanging from fishing line strung across the aisle offered the most privacy. Not many tourists stopped in Rock Creek, but when they did they could get an official Rock Creek T-shirt at Atlas Drugs.

Over the top of a shelf filled with shot glasses and knickknacks, she saw the wide blue and black stripes of his favorite shirt stretched across his broad but youthful shoulders, a young man's shoulders used to carrying the burden of a grown man's responsibilities. He was like that all over—lean and hard with muscle, promising to fill out. For Sarah, everything about Colt was a promise of things to come, of their future.

Sometimes when he looked at her, she saw the deepening of their friendship over the years of a long and good marriage; and sometimes, especially when he'd been kissing her, she saw the heat banked up in him, ready to explode, tethered only by the same love that had lit the fire. It always amazed her, the way he wanted her, and the strength it took not to take her.

As she rounded the edge of a display unit and drew closer to him, she noted the dust on his black cowboy hat and his clothes. His jeans fit him like a soft, well-worn glove, faded indigo hugging narrow hips and strong flanks, and breaking across the tops of remarkably dust-free boots. A smile teased her mouth. She knew the trick. He'd taught her.

"Colt?" she asked softly, not whispering exactly, but not wanting her uncle to hear them. The less her father knew, the better, for all parties concerned.

Colt turned when she spoke, and he felt a small portion of his hurt melt away under the soft gray light of her eyes. There wasn't anyone like Sarah. She wasn't the prettiest girl in town, or the most popular, but he'd had to win her. Once, in grade school, he'd teased her about her straight, dishwater hair until she'd cried, then he'd pulled her braid.

He was still putting his hands on her hair, but only to hold her closer, to feel the silky fine silver and gold strands slip through his fingers. The most he ever did to her braid was unweave it so the summer-blond veil of hair fell over her shoulders. He'd lost count of the number of nights he'd spent dreaming about watching her hair slide over her breasts. It took a lot of imagination. He'd never seen her breasts.

He'd known she was in the aisle, approaching him, but he'd waited to face her, wanting one last chance at pulling himself together just in case something showed. He thought he'd done a pretty good job, until he looked at her.

"Colt?" Her voice went from welcoming to concerned.

He forced a smile and wondered what part of him was giving him away.

"Hi. Can you get out of here?" His voice was gruff, but it didn't shake.

She hesitated for a second, then said, "Sure. Just give me a minute. Do you want a soda?"

He shrugged. "My truck is in the alley."

"I'll be right out."

She brought more than sodas when she came. Her hands were full of cookie and cracker boxes, a few candy bars, and a whole six-pack of cold cola.

She also brought two sandwiches she must have made up in the kitchen in the back. He wondered what her uncle had thought of that.

"You're not letting me eat you out of another paycheck, are you?" He tried to grin again. He could afford a smile now that he had her on his turf. He hadn't felt welcome in the drugstore, because he wasn't welcome anymore. Tobias and he had gotten along real well up until a few weeks ago, when for reasons Colt hadn't understood until today, Sarah's father had told everybody that Colt wasn't supposed to see Sarah any longer, for any reason. Neither he nor Sarah, though, had considered for a minute that they'd give each other up. They'd just gotten careful.

"I'm hungry too," she said, shoving the food across the seat before crawling up into his pickup truck.

Her booted feet had barely left the ground when he scooted over and wrapped his hands around her waist, pulling her across the seat and onto his lap.

"Colton Haines! What do you think you're doing?" She slanted him a provoked glance and reached over to pick up the boxes being crushed by her legs. "You're smashing the creme cookies."

"Kiss me, Sarah." The words were spoken low, with a seriousness that captured her attention.

Her gaze returned to his, and she searched his crystalline-blue eyes, the color of a Wyoming sky, until his dark lashes lowered and his mouth lifted to hers. She met him halfway, not knowing what to expect, but suddenly reminded of the look she'd seen on his face in the drugstore. Colt was hurting.

She kissed him sweetly, her lips soft but closed, and he didn't press for more. But then his hand slid to the nape of her neck, his legs spread apart, and he pulled her between his thighs. That was when the kiss changed, growing mysterious, and darkly exciting, and confusing all at once.

He bit her lips gently, something he'd never done before. His other hand settled on her hip and pulled her closer against him, causing him to groan and her to catch her breath. His mouth came back to hers and he pushed his tongue deep inside, caressing her with slick, even strokes.

Sarah started to tremble, but she couldn't move away. She clung to him, her fingers digging into his shoulders, her mouth open and responsive. She knew what he was doing, what he was pretending to do, but she didn't know where it would lead, not in broad daylight in the alley and not between them, even if they'd been parked on the prairie in the middle of the night.

She couldn't move away, though, and he didn't stop. He only held her tighter. Her breaths grew shallow. His grew rough. She knew when he became aroused, and guilt slipped in next to her confusion and gathering excitement.

"Colt . . . Colt," she whispered, breaking away and burying her face in the crook of his neck.

Colt tilted his head all the way back to the seat, his eyes closed, his teeth clenched. Frustration gnawed on his insides. He was angry, angry at himself for letting go and getting half crude on her, and angry at a nice girl's code when he needed her so badly.

He felt her leave him and slide over to her side of the truck. Her hand came back and rested on his arm in a touch of comfort he didn't acknowledge. He didn't want her young-girl comfort. He wanted the woman inside her. He wanted her beneath him, around him, all over him, until he couldn't think.

"Let's go to the river," he said, and didn't wait for a reply as he pushed himself back behind the steering wheel and started the truck.

The engine was slow to turn over, but Colt was an expert at getting the ancient pickup going and keeping it going. He'd had years of practice and damn little hope of getting a newer or better vehicle. The truck finally fired up, and he pulled out on the prairie side of the alley, to catch the highway on the outskirts of town.

Miles of road and pale amber bluffs ran past them to the horizon, the bluffs breaking into a stretch of cliffs as they neared the river. She was quiet on the other side of the barrier she'd absently built out of boxes of cookies and crackers. She offered him a can of soda, which he accepted without thanks. But he wasn't quiet inside, and he knew what her little wall meant even if she didn't.

He turned off on a dirt track at riverside, following it through two gates and up through the pastures before driving back down to the river. He parked in front of an old barn used officially for winter hay, and unofficially by him and his friend Daniel Calhoun as a fishing shack. Daniel's father owned the ranch, and it was taken for granted that Daniel would own it someday. Colt had often wished his future was as securely mapped out. Instead, it had taken another vicious twist he was going to have to fight damn hard to accommodate.

"Do you want to go swimming?" he asked, the edge still in his voice.

She shook her head, not meeting his eyes. He didn't blame her. He wasn't in much of a mood to face himself either.

He got out of the truck and started for the river, leaving her behind. He'd ground gears getting to her; he'd kissed her as he'd never dared before, he'd dragged her all the way the hell out there—and then he'd walked away. He didn't know what to think.

But he knew he hurt less because she was with him. He knew his thoughts were evening out because she was near, within touching distance if he needed her. He took off his hat and with a snap of his wrist sent it sailing across the pasture to the pussy willows crowding the river.

Sarah watched the black Stetson float through the air and land on a willow branch. When he shrugged out of his shirt and went for his belt buckle, she looked away. She had enough problems without watching him strip down to his underwear. Or so she told herself just before her glance strayed back to where he'd sat down by the riverbank to take off his boots.

Sunlight caught in his white-blond hair and shone along the hard brown length of his arms. His chest was sleekly muscled, his belly ridged and tight. He finished taking off his boots and rose to drop his jeans. She unconsciously held her breath for an instant, capturing her bottom lip with her teeth. The pants came down.

He was hopelessly beautiful, and she loved him beyond reason. The pent-up breath released on a pained sigh. With Colt, the lines between right and wrong grew so damned thin, it was hard to think straight.

Strong legs corded with muscle carried him to the river's edge. His buttocks moved in graceful rhythm beneath the white cotton of his shorts. She watched him dip in and stretch out in the shallows, then kick off and slide deep beneath the water to where the brown trout reigned.

She wanted to know so much about him, everything. She wanted to know how he breathed in his sleep, and what made him so elemental, able to slip into the river and rise again, water flying from his hair, freezing like anybody would, but somehow not minding.

He didn't last too long, though, and soon he was padding back across the strip of pasture between the river and his truck, his shirt flapping open, his jeans damp in spots from his wet legs, his boots hanging from his fingers.

With one lithe movement of bunched biceps and tensed thighs, he levered himself into the back of the pickup, where she had laid out their impromptu picnic.

"Thanks," he said, sitting down and accepting the sandwich she handed him. "You always make the best sandwiches."

It was a compliment of sorts, and Sarah hid her quick grin. Truth was, Colt would eat anything that didn't eat him first, no matter what it tasted like. She was still pleased. For being so crazy in love with him, she had the strangest surge of maternal instincts with him. She didn't want to be his mother—she had enough mothering with four younger brothers—but she sure liked taking care of him.

"How was the river?" she asked.

"Cold." A small smile twitched at the corner of his mouth.

She laughed. "Didn't seem to bother you."

"I'm tough." His gaze caught hers, and the moment of lightness passed. His darkening eyes, filled with a hundred messages, held her motionless beneath the flickering shade and muted sunlight sifting through the cottonwood trees. "I'm leaving, Sarah."

She'd known the words before he'd spoken, and the answer she'd built in her heart was quickly on her lips. "No."

He shrugged and lowered his gaze to take a bite of sandwich.

"No, Colt," she insisted, feeling strong and right. "Nothing can be that bad. There's no reason to leave."

"There's no reason to stay."

She would have hit him for the thoughtless insult, if she could have hit him at all. Instead, she got to her feet, angry and awkward in her haste to get away. He just as quickly pulled her back down, holding her on her knees in front of him. The bed of the truck was hot through her jeans. His hand was tight around her upper arm, his gaze piercing.

"Will you marry me?"

"Yes," she said without hesitation, glaring at him, her anger unabated.

"Will you leave with me?"

"Yes." There was nothing to hold her in Rock Creek except a lifetime of memories, some good, some not so good, and some downright bad. She was signed up for college in the fall, but she wouldn't lose Colt for college. She wouldn't lose him for anything.

"Will you make love with me?" His voice grew more intense, his grip tighter. "Now?"

She stared at him long and hard, then jerked her arm free. "Is this some kind of test?"

He swore and dropped his chin to his chest. When she made a move to leave, he grabbed her again, his hand wrapping around her wrist too tightly for comfort. "No, Sarah. This isn't a test." His lashes slowly lifted, and she saw all his hurt return. "This is real. I want you. I want to make you mine, because I'm leaving and I'm going to lose you."

"You won't lose me, Colt," she promised, her tone softening.

A shuttered look of defeat shadowed his face. "Can't have you. Can't lose you. What in the hell am I supposed to do?"

She felt helpless. "What's wrong, Colt? What's happened?"

"My mom—" He paused and took a steadying breath. "My mom has a new boyfriend."

"Is that so bad?" She didn't understand. If anybody deserved a little happiness, it was Amanda Haines.

"He's married."

"Oh."

"And I think she owes him money." He didn't think it, he knew it. The man was the landlord of his mother's beauty shop, and there was never enough money to spread over the bills.

Dammit all. He worked two jobs besides running their small herd of stock. She could have his money, his school fund. All she had to do was ask.

Or they could sell the damn ranch. It wasn't much of a place to begin with, and once he went to school, they wouldn't be able to keep any stock on it at all.

It took Sarah a minute, but she finally pieced together what he was getting at. The awful truth didn't change her reaction, except to make it sadder.

"I'm sorry, Colt."

His eyes snapped up to hers, flashes of white burning in the cerulean depths. A sneer curled his lips. "My mother is a whore and you're sorry. Thank you."

She would have slapped him then for calling his mother a whore, but he was too fast, rising to his feet. She grabbed his arm instead and stumbled upright to stand in front of him.

"You've got no call to go—"

He silenced her with a quick shake of his head, but had nothing to say—nothing he could choke out around the growing lump in his throat.

Sarah saw the change in him and reacted immediately. "Colt, you've got it all wrong. Hell, half this town is sleeping with the other half, and they're all married to somebody else, and it's not just this town. My aunt who works in a bank in Cheyenne, she says those folks are fooling around all the time."

"It's different when it's your mother." He spoke the words as damning fact, not opinion.

"Different for you," she said. "Not different for your mom. She's just like everybody else, looking for some love."

The look he gave her tore through her with searing heat. "Just like me, Sarah?" he asked, moving closer. "Looking for some love from you?" He slid his hands down over her hips and pulled her tightly against him, claiming her with the action.

"Colt . . ." Her voice trailed off, tremulous.

"Marry me tomorrow," he whispered roughly, lowering his mouth to hers. "But be my wife today."

Two

When he kissed hot and gentle, he was irresistible. His tongue laved and caressed the inside of her mouth, consuming but not devouring, turning tenderness into the pain of wanting and teasing into hungry desire. She responded on instinct alone, parting her lips to taste him more fully, welcoming all of him into her mouth.

Colt held himself in check, dying inside. Kissing her would never be enough. He was already hard.

He broke off the kiss and cupped her face in his hands, holding her gaze with his own. "Daniel and I camped out here over the weekend." Confusion slipped into the passion clouding her eyes. He explained further. "Our sleeping bags are still in the barn, in the loft."

She opened her mouth to speak, but he touched his fingers to her lips.

"Don't say no, not yet. Come with me."

Despite his request, Sarah knew she could say no and he'd take her home. She didn't say no, however, and she didn't analyze why. She didn't dare.

She wanted him. She'd wanted him for years, in the nebulous way girls dreamed about boys. When he'd asked her to the Valentine's Dance, their flirtatious friendship had begun evolving into love. And with his first kiss he'd pushed her nebulous dreams aside, leaving an unfulfilled ache in their place. Months of those kisses had only sharpened her yearnings and clarified exactly what she was aching for. She just didn't know how to take the final step. Saying no was comfortable in its way, familiar. It was a refuge beyond confusion and doubts.

But he'd asked her not to say no, not this time, not yet.

She went with him into the barn, her arm wrapped around his damp waist, his arm draped over her slender shoulder, holding her close with a promise of tenderness. The old structure smelled of the new-mown hay Colt and Daniel had baled and stacked the week before. Dust motes drifted through the rays of light slanting through the weathered and cracked boards.

They went all the way up into the loft. From the open hay door, Sarah could see the blue-gray river running clear and free, the tops of the cottonwood trees flaring out against the sky, and the mountains off in the distance pushing through low clouds.

Behind her, she heard him rolling out the sleeping bags, and a blush burned up her cheeks. She couldn't do this, not even with Colton Haines. She waited for long moments, through the hushed noise of his movements and the silence that followed, building up her courage and the fortitude to say no. She turned.

"Colt, I . . ." The words died on her lips, as soft as the summer breeze ruffling the straight shock of pale hair slanting across his forehead. He was stretched out on the square of padded navy-blue nylon, his body relaxed, yet definitely waiting. One hand cushioned his head and one knee was bent, making a lightninglike pattern of muscular arm, naked torso, and denim-clad leg against the darker cloth. The fingers of his other hand were spread across his lower belly, drawing her attention to the open fastenings of his jeans.

Suddenly Sarah knew it wasn't making love with him that frightened her; it was the thought of never making love with him, or of having him only one time and not having him again. For once she'd given herself to him, the tables would be turned. She knew it without understanding why. She'd be the one holding on to kisses past propriety and prudence. She'd be the one with the hunger inside. She only had to look at him to know the truth.

All his strength was bared for her to see—the flat, taut planes and the work-hardened curves, every flexed muscle beneath the satin sheen of his skin. Watching him breathe was a lesson in the possibilities of perfection in a man's body—and he was offering it all to her.

Her gaze followed the path of least resistance, up from his bare feet to the pulse beating in the hollow of his throat. She'd kissed him there, many times, and stopped herself from letting her mouth slide down to his chest. She wouldn't deny herself again.

She lifted her gaze higher to meet his, and her heart broke at what she saw. His body was all grown up, mature and confident, powerfully male, but the vulnerabilities in his eyes were the essence of youth. The hurt was of a child, and the passion was of a young man who wasn't at all sure he was going to get what he so desperately wanted.

He'd granted her the power to know these things, to care. He wasn't hiding behind the arrogance she'd often seen him use. He hadn't masked his need or his doubts, or his love for her.

She moved away from the barn wall, toward him, one step at a time.

Colt's gaze was riveted to the sway of her hips, the slender length of her legs, and he forced himself not to move, to wait, to let her come to him. Her jeans had flowered cuffs, and flowers on the little triangles of cloth peaking out of the front pockets. The material matched the collar of her pink knit shirt. It was one of the things he thought was so cute about her, the way she was always matched up and proper on the outside, when he knew she was pretty scatterbrained on the inside. She forgot the craziest things, like where she'd left her gloves a minute after she'd taken them off, and to downshift, ever. His last new clutch had been installed in her honor.

She walked through a shaft of sunlight, and the tension in him climbed higher. There was no one like Sarah. She was delicate and strong, sometimes too serious, smarter than anybody else he knew, and beautiful like the fairest of his dreams. Her face was sweetly curved, her skin reminiscent of cream and roses. The gray of her eyes was ever-shifting, full of surprises, yet constant. Her bottom teeth were slightly crooked, and he loved running his tongue over them.

Her mouth knew how to tease him, and often did. Her touch never grew demanding, but he hoped to change that before sunset. He wanted her in ways she probably had never imagined or heard about through whatever grapevine girls used to find out about sex. He wanted to change that too. His most reliable source of knowledge had been a generous older woman, a twenty-seven-year-old barrel racer he'd met the previous summer at a rodeo, who for all her tenderness had never once let him believe he was in love with her.

When Sarah stopped by his side, still standing, he resisted the urge to push himself up and meet her halfway. He wanted her to come to him. He wasn't sure why, but he knew it had more to do with completeness than dominance. He didn't want to undermine her decision with a wrong move, and at this stage, he figured he was in a prime position to make any number of wrong moves.

He'd underestimated her. Sarah sank to her knees besides him, needing little more than his acceptance of what she wanted to give. Her hand drifted across his abdomen, tracing muscles and feeling them tighten in her wake as if she was gathering reins. He moved his hand aside and stretched beneath her caress, granting her his unquestioning compliance.

His skin was warm, with traces of dampness from his swim still slickening his body. Her fingertips glided through the moisture, following a line down the middle of his chest to his navel and the fine dark hair that arrowed beneath his open pants. With only the barest hesitation, she spread her fingers and tunneled them through the silky strands until she held him in her hand.

His body froze. Then slowly, with a soft, ragged breath, he arched into her palm. His response opened the floodgates of a heated, sweet warmth in her and sent it washing through her with tidal strength. His arm came up and pulled her down on top of him, his mouth finding hers with unerring accuracy.

Colt kissed her, forgetting to breathe for long seconds from the pleasure of her touch. He covered her hand with his and held her to him, showing her one way to drive him crazy, and soon he was drawing deep breaths in a rhythm that matched her strokes. When he was sure he couldn't take any more, he captured her wrist with his hand and rolled her beneath him, gentling the kiss.

Sarah moved with him, unresisting, following his lead in the familiar dance.

"I'll never last if we do much more of that." His voice was a rough murmur in her ear, edged with arousal and anticipation.

"I didn't think lasting was the goal," she whispered, and heard his soft laughter in reply.

"For what I want, *lasting* is very important." He lifted his head, and that shock of hair slid down again to hang in front of his eyes. But nothing could disguise or tame the blue fires banked down to his very soul. "I want you, Sarah. I want you to remember me forever, not because I was the first, but because I was the best."

He took her mouth in another sweet pantomime of love that transcended the simplicity of the movements. Everything inside her started to unravel in a slow, unwinding spiral. With each thrust of his tongue, the heat in her body rose toward an inevitable meltdown. He undid the buttons on her shirt and slid his hand around to her back to unclasp her bra. When he didn't find what he was looking for, he lifted his head and gave her a quizzical look.

"French," she whispered, then was both curious and worried when he understood. With a flick of his fingers, he undid the front clasp, and her bra slipped aside.

Colt stared, knowing he never could have imagined such feminine perfection. Descriptions fell over themselves in his mind, tactile words like "creamily soft," "luscious," and "ripe," and words that went straight to his groin, like "sweet on the tongue." He wanted to gaze upon her, and he wanted to touch and caress, but the overriding command was to taste. Lowering his head, he pressed his tongue to her and relished her quick intake of breath.

Honeyed. Deliciously soft and firm. The taste of her breast, the feel of her in his mouth, finally pushed him into the place he'd wanted to be all day—beyond thought.

He slipped to the side of her, kissing her other breast, and began taking off her clothes, pushing her shirt off her shoulders and down each arm. He unzipped her pants with the cute flowered cuffs and sat up to pull them down over her hips, but he only got them and her cotton underwear partway off. His heart tightened at the sight of the soft curls between her thighs. His breath stopped. His chest hurt.

He looked up into her eyes quickly, instinctively

asking for a permission he didn't wait to receive. His breath returned in a sudden rush, and his gaze lowered, along with his mouth.

A shudder racked his body as he nuzzled her and inhaled her sweet female scent. Confusion ran through him like wildfire. He didn't know what to do. He'd felt her body tense beneath him. He was frightening her, he was sure of it, but he couldn't pull away. He tried to remember everything the barrel racer had taught him, but his instincts were a thousandfold more powerful than his memories, guiding him on paths he'd only seen in his dreams.

Shock sizzled through Sarah, along with erotic sensations of dizzying intensity. She clutched at the smooth nylon spread out beneath her. His hand slid up to hold hers, and she was clutching him instead of cloth. He entwined their fingers while he plied bewitchment on her body, his mouth wet and shameless and all over her.

Oh Lord, if she'd known what he was going to do to her, what he *could* do to her, she never would have found the strength to turn him away, not from the very first time he'd kissed her. Every stroke of his tongue turned her to flame. Every time his hand tightened around hers, the revelation of his love rushed through her.

She wanted to call his name. She wanted to sigh it in prayer. She wanted to love him forever and have him always be hers.

Colt could hardly account for what he was doing. Everything was moving so fast inside of him. He was holding her hand, holding her tight, and still coming apart. He slipped his other hand down her leg, pushing her jeans off as he went.

When he got to her boot, he offered a vow of gratitude for the impoverished condition of her footwear. The worn-out ropers were pitifully old, the leather slouched around her ankles, the whole boot stretched out to the point where his slightest tug had her foot free and her jeans half off.

To save himself from finishing before he'd gotten what he wanted, and before he'd had a chance to give all of it back, he moved up her body and captured her mouth. He wished he'd gone ahead and taken his own jeans off, before he'd gotten into the middle of something he didn't want to stop, not even to make it better. But Sarah, sweet Sarah, seemed to know exactly what he needed. With her help and a minimum of interruption, he got rid of his jeans and came back to her, skin to glorious skin—and everything changed.

The urgency was still there, their breathing fast, their bodies painfully restless and in need, but their love, so close to consummation, was now a quieting balm on all the heat and passion.

Colt kissed her mouth with the barest caress of his lips, and her eyes opened, a light suffused gray like the sky before dawn. He smiled.

Taking his time, holding himself against her, he bent her knee so he could reach her other boot and remove it. Her jeans followed, flowers and all, to a pile on the sleeping bag.

Then, and only then, did he push into her, just far enough to watch, with a satisfaction that bordered on arrogance, the dreamy way her eyes drifted closed, her lashes fluttering, her head tilting back.

It wasn't enough.

"Sarah, open your eyes." He pushed deeper and heard her soft, sighing moan.

"I can't, Colt . . . when you do that." But her eyes did slowly open. She wet her lips, her tongue skimming her kiss-bruised mouth in an artless yet utterly provocative gesture.

He reacted physically, without a thought, pressing into her, feeling her give way until she couldn't give way any more. He caught the flare of panic in her eyes, and to save her the added pain of anticipation, he thrust.

It was heaven, it was coming home. He held himself still, kissing her wantonly to keep from doing anything else, giving her time to adjust. But the time he stole for gallantry was short-lived. Soon his body moved, slowly, with deliberation, then moved again, settling into a potently seductive rhythm. He couldn't help himself. But he could help her, and he did, touching her in well-taught ways, until between the heat and the rhythm and the sheer pleasure of friction, the girl he loved became a woman in his arms, her sweet gasps echoing in his ears, his name on her lips.

The tight, wet heat of her pulsing around him tore through him, compelling him to thrust deeper, thrust harder. The sounds of her sent him surging upward, chasing her release with the building intensity of his own. The scent of her, female, sweet, and musky, the taste she'd left on his lips, infused his senses, imprinted her indelibly on all of his body.

Climaxing amidst such wonder humbled and exalted him, left him spent and weakened, yet immeasurably stronger, for now she was his.

Sarah.

He gathered her in his arms and held her, kissing her face and listening to her words of love, until with a naturalness he'd expected, he was hard and ready for her again.

Sarah felt him rocking against her, felt his kisses change from sweet to serious, and she welcomed him to her once more. She was sore and achy, but he had her swollen with need, and she wasn't willing to miss even a single chance at the heaven she'd found when he was deep inside her, filling her with his body, with his needs, with his love.

The boy-turned-man was sweet passion incarnate in her arms, giving her everything with his shameless mouth and powerful young body. She was enough of a woman to recognize the gift of her own pleasure, and enough in love with him to want to return the gift in any way she could.

Afternoon slipped to dusk, stealing sunlight from the sky while they sought the depths of sensation and satiation within each other. She caressed him everywhere with her tongue, gently biting the soft skin of his inner thigh, sweetly ministering where he begged for her touch.

When the coolness of evening began its steady intrusion into their sensual idyll, they got half dressed and lay down to watch the last shades of sunset fade from the sky. Wrapped in the warmth of each other's arms, they accepted what they had become: lovers and mates, the keen edge of excitement on each other's lives, two people sharing a haven of dreams and love.

"Sarah." He whispered her name like an invocation, brushing his face against the side of her neck, inhaling the fragrance of their lovemaking and the sweet melange of scents that were uniquely hers. He wasn't going anywhere. He couldn't leave her, not after this. It would take everything he had just to leave her this night.

He opened his mouth in a soft kiss on her skin. How long, he wondered, would it take to get enough of her? And was it a love even deeper than he'd realized that now made him want to throw roses at her feet? Dark red roses, full-blown and heavy with perfume, petals lush and open, the way she'd been for him. And pink roses, budded and infinitely fragile, with all the innocence she'd given.

It had to be the overwhelming love he felt, he decided between gentle kisses and deep breaths of bone-deep satisfaction. Where else would a twenty-year-old cowboy from Rock Creek, Wyoming, get a vision of such fanciful eroticism? He didn't know. He couldn't remember ever thinking about flowers before, at least not in conjunction with a woman's body—and he'd done his share of thinking about women's bodies.

He bent his head to kiss her again, but got no further than the barest touch of his mouth on hers, when his attention was arrested by a flash of light on the far wall. He rolled over on one elbow and saw the light again, flickering through the cracks in the barn wallboards.

"Get dressed, Sarah. Someone's coming." He wasn't too worried. It was probably Daniel. He shrugged into his shirt and started doing up the snaps, then stopped to do up her buttons instead, smiling and teasing her with quick kisses.

"Colt, don't," she said between laughs as she realized that for every button he was fastening, he was unbuttoning another. "We'll never get anywhere with you—"

Her words were cut short by the crashing open of the barn door. The glare of truck headlights poured in on the bottom floor, illuminating the blocked shadows of bales of hay, and a voice rang out in a bellow of rage.

"Sarah!"

Colt's blood ran cold, and he felt Sarah turn to ice beneath his hands. They were both frozen in fear, but for Colt, the fear was quickly replaced by rage. His mother's caller had come to call on him.

Paralysis crawled to the tips of Sarah's fingers and turned her muscles to lead. Her breath wouldn't come. Heavy footsteps sounded in the dirt below, and her father hollered again.

"Sarah!"

She wanted to flee, but there was no place to go. With even more urgency, she wanted Colt to run. Her throat was tight, though, too tight to force his name through. It was too late, anyway, for he was already moving down the ladder, going only a couple of steps before jumping to the ground to face his adversary.

She scrambled after him, panicked, sobs welling in her throat and almost choking her. She knew her father, too well. She'd seen him fight with other men. It was practically a Friday night family tradition, going to a bar and sitting quiet in a corner while her dad got drunk and mean and her mom got worried and scared.

"Where's my girl, boy? What have you done with her?"

Sarah heard her father locate Colt in the shadows below the loft, his voice deathly calm. Her foot stilled on the top rung.

"She's not yours anymore, Bull. She's mine." His voice cut through the tension like the edge of a blade.

Sarah gripped the poles of the ladder, squeezing her eyes shut to fight her sudden anger at Colt. Didn't he know he was provoking a rattler? Her father could strike so fast, lash out and hurt with a speed what was as frightening as the pain he delivered—and that was without the bullwhip that had earned him his sobriquet.

"Dad . . ." She drew in a shallow breath. "I'm up here. I'm coming down."

The scraping noise of her boots touch-tapping and slipping off the wooden rungs of the ladder was the only sound in the barn. She reached the dirt floor and cast a quick glance at Colt, then had to look away before she buckled under the accusations in his eyes. He was wrong. She wasn't choosing sides. She was choosing to save him. She knew there was no saving herself from her father's anger.

A fresh surge of fear almost made her run to Colt and cling to him. Then her courage returned. Her father had never actually hit her, not like he did her mother. He threatened and yelled. He'd back her into a corner and make her cower, but he had never landed a blow, just as he never laid a hand on his young sons.

She doubted if he'd be as considerate or "gentle" with Colt, especially if Colt insisted on standing up to him. Nothing made him angrier than a show of backbone when he was in a beating mood, and

Colt had more backbone than most. And less sense, if he thought he could take on her father.

"Colt, go home." She made her own stand, but it was as if she were invisible to the two men. Neither of them acknowledged her shakily given command.

"The boy and I are going to have a talk," her father said.

"Damn straight." If possible, Colt's voice was even angrier than her father's.

Sarah looked at her father. He wasn't a big man, but he was hard and uncompromising. His hands were used to tightening into fists. Gray touched his hair, but it had come early. He wasn't old, not nearly old enough to give Colt an age advantage. Quite the contrary. Sarah thought any age advantage went to her father, along with any experience advantage. He'd been brawling in bars since before she was born. Colt had never been in a bar or a brawl in his life, not as far as she knew.

The sound of another car approaching had all three of them glancing toward the door.

"That'll be your uncle," Bull said. "Get, girl."

"I'm not going anywhere." Lord help her, she prayed, her suddenly parched lips moving soundlessly. There she was, showing her backbone. Her stomach knotted up, and a stitch grew in her side. Her palms started to sweat. She hated herself for being such a coward. "Not without Colt."

A door slammed outside.

"Toby!" her father barked. "Get in here and get Sarah out!"

Her uncle appeared in the barn door, looking like he wished he was anywhere else on the planet besides standing in that barn, under the perpetual, unforgiving thumb of his older brother.

"Come on, Sarah. Let's go." Toby started toward her, and she took a step back. He stopped, meeting her gaze with steady but hopeless determination. Colt moved, too, and her father intercepted him, blocking the younger man's way in a standoff.

She was cornered. She was scared. Her gaze darted between the three men, and in the split second that she took her eyes off her uncle, he grabbed her. She struggled against his encircling arms, and they tightened, lifting her off the ground.

"Hush, child," he said quietly in her ear, sliding his hand over her mouth to silence the scream building in her throat. "Hollering is only going to get him riled."

He hauled her out into the night, despite her fighting and squirming. She stared wildly back at the barn and the twin pools of light cocooning Colt and her father against the dark shadows.

From inside the barn, Colt heard the car pull away. He allowed himself a quick glance into the night to confirm her leaving. Bull went to his truck, and Colt immediately returned his attention to the older man, watching him carefully. He was glad Sarah was gone. What needed to be said between her father and him didn't need to be heard by her. Bull Brooks could talk all night long and never convince him of a damn thing, but Colt wasn't leaving until Bull understood that he should stay away from his mother. And that Sarah was his, no compromises.

A strange flickering movement next to the older man caught Colt's eye, and he realized Bull had no intention of talking. He'd pulled something off the gun rack in his truck, and it was snaking across the ground, through the dirt and the chaff, looking alive and deadly.

Colt swore under his breath, filling the harsh syllable with equal measures of fear and disbelief. Then a snapping crack resounded through the air, and pain sliced across his skin.

Three

A quartet of quavering female voices rose and fell with the plaintive phrases of the hymn, matching the changeable weather blowing past the high church windows. A thunderstorm was building up on the plains, biding its time before it would roll over Rock Creek in a torrent of sound and glory.

A thunderstorm rolling over Rock Creek. Sarah had expected it. She'd been expecting it for days, ever since Amanda Haines had succumbed to a weak heart. Colt was coming home, ten years too late to make a damn bit of difference, ten years too late for her to care.

But God, how she hurt for him.

She smoothed her fingers over the worn white-leather cover of her Bible, feeling the pain and loss of the past, remembering the nights she'd soaked the Bible's pages with her grief, her unanswered prayers. He shouldn't have left the way he did, without a word, after stealing every ounce of love she had in her heart.

She knew where he'd gone: to his uncle in California. She knew what he'd done: joined the Navy. She knew what he'd become: part of a SEAL team, the best. But she'd heard none of it from him. He lived in bits and pieces of gossip, in a decade of stray comments voiced in Atlas Drugs.

Her hand slipped to the black poly-cotton of her simple homemade dress. Wasn't she a sight? Sitting in church, mourning the death of her father's mistress. Or did people even use that word anymore? She didn't know. Rock Creek wasn't exactly on the cutting edge of society's mores, and she seldom went anywhere else, not that any of it mattered. She'd liked Amanda Haines. Her parents had divorced years ago. Her mother had taken her young sons and found a man who knew how to love without hitting. Bull and Amanda had seen each other on and off through the years, and one day it had struck Sarah like a bolt of lightning—what had broken Colt's heart that day so many years ago.

She'd hated her father for a long time after that, until she'd grown tired of expending her energy on his worthless hide. He still owned every damn thing in town, and she paid him her rent on the drugstore. To the best of her ability, she limited their relationship to that. Her mother lived close enough to keep her from feeling like an orphan, if such a feeling was possible for a grown woman— which, of course, it was.

She sighed and opened her hymnal, then rose to sing with the rest of the congregation. Most everyone had turned out for Amanda Haines's funeral, which was only right. The additional voices lifted the singing to new heights, providing volume and steadiness. Sarah let the song sweep her along, her thoughts floating between catching the right note and riding it to the end, and pictures of Amanda, whose greatest contribution to Sarah's life had been not looking like her son. She couldn't have borne that, facing those eyes like the Wyoming sky across the prescription counter. For she'd been right: Her greatest fear in making love to Colt had been not having him again. She'd prayed for his return and been denied. She'd prayed for his child and had none. She'd known a few other men, much to her disappointment. He'd ruined her, not by stealing her virginity, but by stealing her trust. It had left her incomplete and unable to love another.

Damn him. She wasn't ready for him to return. Ten years wasn't nearly long enough.

She lifted her voice to meet the chorus and in mid-note stopped cold. Pemonition warned her a second before thunder cracked and tore across the sky, shaking the walls. Her heart beat faster, too much faster, while everyone kept on singing as if nothing had happened. Her breath caught in her throat as the first murmurs reached her ears from the back of the church.

So sorry. So sorry . . . too long . . . anything you need. Good to see you . . . bad circumstances.

Lightning flashed close, throwing stark illumination into the sanctuary and supercharging the air into another explosion of sound.

Welcome home . . . so sad . . . a good woman. Gonna miss her . . . the whole town . . . you know. So sorry . . . so sorry, Colton.

He was there, moving closer with each hushed sound, and she couldn't have turned around to save her life. It was too much to expect, her having to face him ever.

She gripped the hymnal, tiny tendons straining all the way up the back of her hand. Thunderheads full of nature's promised glory rolled over Rock Creek in a wash of water, driving rain against the dust and the clapboard church as he stopped right next to her in the aisle.

His shoes were black and shiny like pools of liquid wax, mesmerizing. With a carefully calibrated lift of her lashes she followed a knife-edge crease of navy-blue twill up long, rigid legs. A broad hand held the white hat of a Navy officer by his side. The size of him had increased with age. His shoulders went on forever, broad and muscular beneath his tailored dress uniform. He was so stiff, all his muscles frozen at attention. When her gaze reached the pulse point in his neck, she got her first remembrance of the boy she used to know. There the lifeblood beat heavy and strong and vital. She dared go no farther. Her nerves were fraying a thread at a time, right down to the fibers; her heart was still beating too fast.

He turned his attention to her at that moment, his chin lining up with her gaze, and the compelling force of him drew her on.

The hymn swirled around them, praising the Lord for His mercies. A hundred bodies filled the small church, a hundred voices, and a hundred other thoughts. Nothing touched her except Colt—the squared line of his jaw, so much more angular than it had been, the hardness around his mouth and the scar on his chin, neither of which had been present when she'd loved him. His nose was more familiar, the short slope and slight uptilt on the end, but his whole countenance had been chiseled by the years, honed down to the basics of leanness and strength.

Her final error proved fatal: the lifting of her gaze to his eyes. The Wyoming sky had never been bluer, or so empty. No flicker of memory cast a shadow on his eyes. He was Medusa, turning her to stone.

She nodded, her own body suddenly as stiff as a Navy lieutenant at attention in his dress uniform, and she turned back to her hymnal, picking up the song on the second refrain. She'd known she wasn't ready, and he'd proved the fact beautifully. How awful.

He moved on, joining his relatives in the first pew. But he didn't blend in. Nothing about him resembled either the citizens of Rock Creek or his own flesh and blood. None of them had his warrior's elegance, the discipline that kept his body straight and tall, even with his head bowed in prayer.

Funny, she thought, how slowly time was suddenly passing. For an eternity, she studied his broad back and the neatly trimmed hair at the nape of his neck. His hair was darker, not as silvery but more golden, darkly golden. He tilted his head to one side, toward his paternal grandmother, and Sarah's brows instantly knitted. Her pulse picked up with a simultaneous infusion of adrenaline.

Good Lord, what had happened to him? Had someone tried to slit his throat and missed? She stared and tried not to imagine how he'd gotten the scar that sliced across the side of his neck. When he dipped his head lower to whisper something to his grandmother, she realized it continued on to his nape. But when he straightened, the white line cutting across his skin disappeared beneath his starched collar.

Her heart suddenly beat more heavily in her chest. She was even less ready than she'd imagined, less ready than he'd proved. Fortunately, lots of people cried at funerals, and no one would guess her tears were provoked by anything other than an appropriate grief. She knew, though, and the truth horrified her. Crying for him at this late date, after the empty look he'd given her. She obviously had emotions that had never heard the word pride.

At the end of the service, she slipped out with half a dozen other ladies to put the finishing touches on the supper in the church basement. Amanda would be remembered with love and friendship, and with casseroles and cakes. Her son would be greeted and condolences would be given by one and all, including herself. Nothing could shake her sense of duty and propriety, not even Colton Haines.

She'd take her time. She'd regroup and find another way to steel herself, but the words would be spoken, words of compassion and respect. It was one of the ways people survived. She wouldn't deny him his due.

As Colt stood by his mother's casket, he clasped another hand, and then another. He greeted most people by name. That was all—just their names. They poured out their heartfelt clichés, though some tried for more, especially the women. He answered with their names and tried not to feel anything, not the welcome they offered and certainly not the comfort. Comfort implied pain, and he wasn't ready for the pain.

His mom had been fine at Christmas when she'd spent a week out in California with him, and at fifty-five she'd been far too young to die from heart failure. Whatever the hell that meant.

Tension tightened his jaw, making it impossible for him to get out the next few names—Ed, Charlie, Roberta. He knew them all, every one, and none of them had called to tell him his mom was sick. The doctor had said he'd tried a week ago, but Colt had been on the other side of the world a week ago, saving somebody else's life.

"Mrs. Childress." He spoke the preacher's wife's name and held her small, weak hand in his. Wisps of gray hair floated out of her coiled bun, giving her a softly electrified appearance.

She patted his arm and gripped him tightly, as if holding on to him would stop the perpetual trembling of her hands, or as if she could support his young man's body with her old woman's spirit.

"She went quickly, child. No pain. We tried to contact you so many times, but you are a very difficult person to find."

Colt wanted to stop her right there. He needed his anger. He didn't want a kindly soul to take away the only emotion he trusted.

"It's my job," he said, his voice as empty as the rest of him. Then he wished he hadn't spoken, especially so rudely to the preacher's wife.

She misunderstood, though, disallowing even his anger at himself.

"We're all very proud of you, Colton, of all our

service boys. We know it's a difficult job, defending the country. We're very appreciative."

He'd meant it was his job to be hard to find. And he doubted if any of Rock Creek's other "service boys" had seen his kind of action. He hoped not. Some of the things he'd done he wouldn't wish on his enemies, let alone a Wyoming cowboy. But he had, of course, wished the wildest, most carefully constructed worst-case scenarios of the United States government on his faceless enemies and bent them to his will through force and cunning, through speed, surprise, and the ability to disappear.

He was good, maybe too good.

Doris Childress squeezed his hand and moved on to his grandmother. He had two uncles and an aunt there, too, but he was having a hard time finding anything to say to anybody. He'd come back for his mother, out of love and respect, despite their differences, despite the man she'd loved. He'd never told her anything to tarnish her dream.

Robert "Bull" Brooks was in the church. Colt had seen him, but the older man wouldn't meet his gaze, or even look in his direction. Smart man. Colt had forgotten nothing, and he'd learned a hundred ways to maim and kill. Bull knew only one. He must also know that half his protection had passed away with Amanda.

Amanda . . . Colt closed his eyes. He'd always loved her name, and she'd loved that bastard. At least five more emotions tangled themselves up in the mess that was his heart—another kind of anger, an unslaked need for vengeance, disgust, shame, and a sense of injustice. He'd felt them all for ten years, and fought them all. But his mother had died and everything inside him was opening up, no matter what he did to keep it under control.

The storm was worsening, darkening the sky, when they returned to the church from the cemetery. Colt had wanted to call it quits right then and there, with the dirt falling on his mother's grave, but leaving hadn't been an option. He had to face the whole thing from beginning to end like the officer he was. He had to stick to the plan, without screwups. Forward was the only allowable direction.

Still he hesitated at the top of the church steps. Wind whipped the rain into his eyes and across his cheeks, but it went unnoticed by a man used to salt spray at twenty knots and free-falls from four miles up.

Forward meant Sarah. If he went forward, he'd have to face her again. He swore under his breath.

She should have changed more than she had. She should have cut her hair. Age should have changed the gray of her eyes. She should be taller or fatter, less gentle, less inviting. She shouldn't be able to look at him and make him hurt.

His grandmother continued into the church, and he automatically moved forward to keep his supporting hand on her elbow. His moment of hesitation was over, his last chance gone.

The church kitchen was a maelstrom of activity: twenty hot dishes, ten salads, assorted vegetables, five cakes, and seven women shuffling it all from oven and microwave to table. Sarah knew when Colt walked into the basement, her eyes unerringly lifting from where she was cutting Paula Jenk's double-fudge cake.

She forced her gaze back down. She'd served a dozen remembrance suppers, and she'd serve one more before she gave him the speech she'd been stumbling over for the last hour. The one about being so sorry, about how wonderful his mother had been, about if there was anything he needed—though she'd make sure she said that part just right, with a vacuous, saccharine quality he'd surely be smart enough to understand meant he shouldn't ask—about how good it was to see him.

No . . . no. She'd decided against that part completely. She'd tell him it was good to have him home in Rock Creek, using that same vacuous expression that acted like a wall against any real feeling. Above all, she had to avoid real feeling.

And timing. Timing was another key to a smooth condolence. There would be a crush of good-byes after the supper, and she'd shove herself forward in the middle of it, making it clear she'd tried hard to get to him. She'd speak her short piece and politely let herself be shoved aside, maybe with a lift of her shoulders or her eyebrows to let him know how sorry she was they couldn't have talked longer.

More the fool she for believing in best-laid plans. The supper got completely away from her, with her running back and forth from the kitchen to the serving area, and a couple of mild catastrophes, when the coffee urn stopped in mid-perk and then when some little kid, one of the Barton boys, accidentally sent the fudge cake crashing to the floor, though luckily after most of it had been served.

A hundred people ate, and Sarah barely saw a one of them. She got frosting on her knees from the cake cleanup. Every time she turned around it seemed she was brushing coffee grounds off her dress, or she'd put a run in her stockings. But the worst, the absolute worst, was when she finally got everything under control, the supper was over. She came out of the kitchen to find the basement practically empty. The Women's Auxiliary was still in full force, tidying up the dining area, but the townspeople had dispersed . . . and taken Colton Haines with them.

She was crushed, instantly and totally. Her shoulders lowered into a confused, rag doll slump. She looked again, from corner to corner, even behind her, as tears and a surprising panic rose up.

He was gone.

A lump thickened in her throat. Her facial muscles gave up all semblance of tone and structure, and her lower lip trembled. He was gone. The wound was ten years old, but the pain was as sharp as a cut from a knife.

Her life was such a wasteland. No lover, no husband, no family of her own. It wasn't supposed to have been like that.

He'd come home for the first time in ten years, and she'd wasted all her time concocting face-saving speeches. Somebody ought to take her out and shoot her, but nobody would, not in Rock Creek. They needed her to dole out their medicines and give advice and first aid—and she needed something else, *somebody* else. A soft, quick sob broke from her. She was going to cry right there, maybe have a whole breakdown, and she didn't give a damn who saw her.

The first tear was already halfway down her cheek before she covered her face with one hand and wrapped her other arm around her waist. Then she heard it, a voice unlike any other, deeper, stronger, for all its quietness.

She lifted her head and wiped her cheek, relief flooding her veins and pushing her toward that voice. Mike Clymer saw her coming and finished up talking with Colt, giving her the chance for a private moment of shared sorrow with the hometown hero. A few seconds passed between Mike's departure and her entrance into the hall where the two men had been talking, and in those seconds all of her doubts returned. She wasn't going to change her mind about talking to him, but she couldn't remember what she was supposed to say.

Mike's work boots sounded on the stairs, covering her own soft tread. Colt was momentarily alone in the basement hallway, and the sudden change in him made her doubts pale once more. He looked completely lost, worn out, and ready to bolt.

She quickly closed the distance between them, drawing his attention. The instant he saw her all his defenses went back into place like clockwork—the shuttered look in his eyes, the straightening of his spine, the squaring of his jaw. But not before she caught a glimpse of recognition and panic.

Panic. She was sure of it. The Navy SEAL was afraid of her. She didn't find the knowledge particularly encouraging.

Colt fixed his eyes on Sarah, not believing his

damn rotten luck. He'd been so close to getting out of there.

She started in by saying all the things he'd been hearing for the last three hours, except she was stammering more than most. Somehow her pauses and hesitations gave the sentiments a deeper sincerity. She was sorry, of course. Everyone was sorry. His mother had been a wonderful woman. God, did they think he didn't know that?

So damn close. His military jeep was less than thirty feet away, parked right outside the door at the top of the stairs. If he closed his eyes, he could see his hand on the key in the ignition, turning it, the wheels rolling backward, and the highway stretching all the way to Cheyenne and escape. He could be back in California before nightfall, chasing the sun into the Pacific Ocean with a bottle of Scotch.

He opened his eyes, nodding, pretending the lapse had been nothing more than an extended blink and not a desperate bid for freedom. She should have changed. It was an unnecessary cruelty for her to be so much the same as he'd always remembered. *Always.*

Her hair shouldn't be the same silky silver and gold. He'd never seen anything like it, and he'd seen everything else in California. But no amount of sun and sea and potions could equal Sarah's natural coloring.

He remembered how it felt to wrap her hair in a gentle fist and draw her near. He remembered the feel of the soft strands sliding over his bare arm, caressing his shoulder and falling across his chest. He remembered the one night he'd held the long veil aside to gaze upon her breasts, so perfect, so perfectly sweet.

He remembered too much.

He forced his gaze back to her eyes, but he knew he wouldn't last long with those fathomless gray lakes measuring him from the inside out. He tried a quick glance at her mouth and was captured nonetheless.

She'd stopped stammering, though he'd lost all track of what she was saying. He tried concentrating.

"I still had a year of school when Tobias left, but the town muddled through until I got my pharmacist's license. I was lucky they didn't get too used to going into Cheyenne."

She was telling him her life story, and he was fascinated by the curve of her mouth, the way her lips formed words, and the occasional glimpse of her tongue. In the long run that seemed a safer area of attention than her words.

She wasn't married. She didn't come out and tell him, but neither did she mention a man, or say anything that matched her up with someone. There wasn't a "we" in her story. No children either. He knew enough about women to know their children always figured into a conversation pretty quick. It was natural. It was right.

Sarah didn't have a man, and she didn't have children, and there lay his true shame. It wasn't that Bull Brooks had whipped him for making love to his daughter, but that he'd left her in Rock Creek alone.

How far away was his jeep? Thirty feet? Ten stairs and a few yards?

And how would he get there? Snap his hat on

his head and do an about-face? Turn away from those soft eyes and the sweet curves of her mouth as she talked to him about tax incentives for a feedlot that in the end they were sure they were going to lose to Albany County.

His fingers tightened on the brim of his hat. His gaze drifted over the swells of her breasts, over her still boyishly slim hips. She should have changed there. Bearing children should have changed her there.

He uttered a foul obscenity. He wasn't any good at this. He shouldn't have come. He shouldn't have stayed long enough to feel the pain. Another curse lodged against his clenched teeth.

She gave him a startled glance. "Well, it's not all that bad, really. We've voted in Peter Barton as mayor, and with him being into real estate sales, we're sure he'll try to develop Rock Creek to its fullest potential."

His chest was getting too tight for him to breathe. It was an odd feeling, thoroughly miserable, and it meant something he couldn't quite remember.

Damn her. She knew what was happening and responded in the worst possible manner. She touched him, her fingers light on his sleeve; she spoke his name, filling the syllable with compassion and her woman's tenderness.

He wasn't ready for it, for any of it. He wasn't ready for her. Thirty feet?

He'd never make it.

"Colt?"

She did it again, so sweetly, with such yearning, and all the walls inside him started to shake and tremble. His ramparts were crumbling.

His eyes drifted closed and his head lowered in

pained resignation. He felt her move a step closer, felt the air change with her nearness, with her scent, with her softness invading him. A rational man would have taken a great leap for the stairs. Colt didn't move.

The last losing seconds of the battle raged inside him, all but forgotten as he raised his lashes and fell headlong, drowning, into the sanctuary of her eyes. He lifted his hand and found her waist. The small of her back filled his palm and he applied a gentle, insistent pressure. She didn't resist, and all he wanted was to survive the moment. He did what had to be done. He kissed her.

Sarah. *Sarah.* . . .

Four

He opened his mouth over hers, his tongue pressing for immediate entrance. There were no hesitations in his heart. He needed her to hold him, to hold him together, and he'd take everything she didn't tie down.

Sarah was captured within the iron circle of his arms, pinned between his body and her need, absolutely paralyzed by the rush of sensation flooding her.

It had been terrible: his silence, the grim line of his mouth, and her rattling on about every inconsequential thing that popped into her mind. She'd gotten no reading off him at all until she mentioned the feedlot, and that for some reason had upset him—a mild reaction when compared to the near devastation she'd seen in his eyes when she'd mentioned that Peter Barton was the new mayor.

She'd obviously missed something. Nobody cared that Peter Barton was mayor, not even the people

who'd voted for him. She'd definitely missed something, and she'd figure it out—she promised herself she would—just as soon as she stopped dying
in his arms, as soon as her feet found the earth, as
soon as he slowed down from the sweet, torturous
ravishment of her mouth.

Just don't let it be over too soon. The thought
rolled over and over in her mind as she let herself
sink against him, into him. She was ashamed of
herself. She wanted to cry for needing him so
much, the taste of him, the feel of him. But no
other man's kisses had touched her so deeply,
and her heart reached for him.

She'd get over him. And she wouldn't let him
kiss her forever. Just close to forever, just until
she was filled with him, with Colton Haines.

She had changed. Colt felt it. Her body was
stronger, more of a match for him, molding to him
with heat and need. She was fuller, her mouth
intensely sweeter for being less chaste. He remembered that long-ago night, tasting himself on
her lips and tongue, and what it had done to him
then. He felt what kissing her was doing to him
now.

There were other changes, too, disturbing
changes. The hint of desperation in her filled him
with guilt. He wanted to kiss the desperation
away. He was so sorry. He should have understood.

The smartest girl he'd ever known, the one he'd
loved, had never figured out how to compromise.
She'd never learned how to take affection and mix
it with lust and somehow almost convince herself
that it was love. He doubted if she'd found much
pleasure without at least the semblance of love.

Sometimes making love was such an emptiness. He'd never wanted that for her, not from the very beginning. He'd wanted her to know only him and the way he'd loved her the first time, with care and tenderness and all the passion he'd been able to imagine and make.

He'd been his best for her, given her more than he'd given any other woman. Kissing her in the church basement now made him want to give it to her all over again, the way he'd dreamed for a thousand nights after he'd left, until he'd learned how to compromise enough to get by without seeing her face every time he made love to someone else.

He moved his hand to cup her face, his fingers and palm following the delicate contour of her jaw and tunneling into her hair, a selfish gesture he couldn't resist. He'd noticed in the church how she'd fixed her hair into big, loose curls, and he'd noticed later at the serving tables how the curls had fallen out, her hair still refusing to cooperate.

He wanted to love her. He gently gnawed on her mouth, pulled away and ended the kiss, then came back for a deeper taste. Her breath shuddered and sighed against his lips when he finally lifted his head. Her eyes remained closed.

He stroked her soft cheek with his thumb. "Come with me to the Regent." His voice was rough, with an emotion he recognized only as need.

The Regent? The Regent Motel? Sarah opened her eyes. He knew every secret in her heart, every thrill coursing through her veins. He knew how badly she wanted him.

All she could do was stare and not cry. Then all she could do was stare.

She jerked away and took two steps, stopping when the damn tears spilled onto her cheeks. He was going to leave if she walked away; she knew it beyond doubt. Leave her right there in the church basement, and this time he'd never come back.

Why? she wondered, her hands constricting into tight fists, her tears tracing dampness on her cheeks. Why did she have to be a complete and total fool to even get a chance to talk with him? It wasn't fair.

She took another step.

"Don't go, Sarah."

She stiffened under the touch of his hand on her arm, under the gruff caress of his voice. What was he going to do now? Kiss her again? Ruin her life? What had he been thinking to kiss her in the first place? She'd been giving him her condolences and ten years' worth of life history. She'd made a point of doing nothing, saying nothing, not even thinking anything that might remind him of what they had once been. She'd tried to play fair, and he'd cheated right down to the core.

What did he want? she thought angrily. Besides the obvious.

She forced herself to move again, but his hand tightened.

"I'm sorry," he said. A second passed, then another before his hand fell away.

"I have to finish cleaning up." She didn't look back at him.

"I'll wait."

Fine. He'd wait, and she'd try to figure out what in the world she'd do when the waiting was over.

• • •

Colt sucked a short swallow off his bottle of
Scotch and chased it with a longer draw off his
beer. He wasn't drunk, not even close, but the fact
that liquor lowered body temperature was becoming a noticeable reality.

He leaned forward and turned on the ignition,
running the heat to get the chill out of the jeep.
The rain hadn't let up. The thunder still rolled.
Lightning played cat and mouse through the tow-
ering banks of clouds filling up the sky. It was a
hell of a night to be sitting in a parking lot in a
jeep, waiting for salvation and a woman.

The back door of the church opened, and after a
quick check to make sure it wasn't Sarah, he went
back to watching the grass get wet on one hundred and eighty degrees of horizon. He'd missed
Wyoming more than he'd realized, all the beautiful
nothingness.

He stretched back into the seat and wet his
tongue with the Scotch, just enough to taste and
give an edge to his beer. He was pacing himself. He
had the whole night to get through, and he didn't
want to do it in a stupor.

He wanted to do it in Sarah's arms, in her bed.
Wanting her gave him a focus he wasn't about to
forfeit, no matter how long she made him wait in
the cold rain.

He didn't know if it was possible to still love her
the way he had. It didn't seem likely. But he knew
he wanted her with the same intensity. The moti-
vating force was more calculated than desperate,
but the need was the same. He'd found solace and
heaven with her once, and he'd wait all night on

even the off chance of finding it again. He wasn't falling apart any longer. He was solidifying, and it was in a place he didn't want to be.

He tilted the bottle once again.

He still thought her beautiful, though he knew other men might not. Daniel had always dismissed her as cute in an offbeat way. A couple of the guys on his SEAL team wouldn't even notice her, but they were the younger ones, the ones who still kept their brains below their belts, which wasn't all bad. For some of the things he'd asked them to do, not thinking too much was a distinct advantage. The older guys, like Rick and Boomer and Garrett, they'd know right off that she was special without him saying a word.

The church door opened again, drawing his attention, and suddenly Colt was glad none of his friends were around to offer unsolicited opinions or get in the way. He jumped out of the jeep and came around to get her, not wanting her to mistake for a second where she belonged.

He shrugged out of his coat and threw it over her shoulders, tucking her under his arm as he did. She fit there so perfectly. He held her close against the blowing wind and the showering rain.

She balked slightly at the door to the jeep, but he pretended not to notice, instead expending a nominal amount of force to guide her inside, more a tensing of his muscles than a true exertion of strength.

It was enough. She slipped into the seat and he shut the door behind her.

The first thing Sarah noticed was the bottle of Scotch balanced between the driver's seat and the gearshift; the second was the half-empty six-pack of beer at her feet. Before she could decide how concerned she should be, he got in and pulled his door closed.

Water ran down the side of his face and followed the line of his jaw to the shallow cleft in his chin. He wiped the rain away with a lift of his shoulder, never taking his eyes off her.

Tension rose inside her. He was a stranger. Except for the way he'd kissed her, she didn't know him.

His white shirt was soaked through, shrink-wrapped to the hard muscles in his arms and the breadth of his shoulders. He'd loosened his tie and unbuttoned both his collar and the next button. Not enough to incite a riot, but enough to affect her. The inside of the jeep was so small, not really big enough for two people and all their memories.

"Can I take you somewhere for dinner?" It was the straightest question Colt could formulate, a standard line designed to keep female quarry from running off before a man had a chance to prove the simple sincerity behind his intentions. Not that women often bought the simple sincerity behind wanting to get lost in the act of making love, in simply coming together physically as intensely as possible.

"We just had supper."

He was a mess and she wanted to be practical. He took a deep breath, still holding her with his gaze.

"How about a drink?"

She gave the bottle of Scotch a quick glance and flushed slightly.

"A *mixed* drink." He'd play the game all night long if he had to. She wasn't going to shake him.

She turned to look out the window, her lips squeezed together, her eyes wide, and he was shook all right, down to the pit of his stomach and the soles of his shoes.

Anger and frustration shot through him in one searing bolt. "*My God*, Sarah. Where do you want me? On my knees?"

She didn't say a word, and the only acknowledgment she gave his plea was the tear that ran down her face.

He swore under his breath and jammed the jeep into gear. "I'll take you home. Where do you live?"

She gave him directions, and he wheeled the jeep around. This, then, was the best after all, he thought. Cheyenne and escape. There was too much going on in Rock Creek, more confusion than he needed or wanted. She was a dream he couldn't have, not reality.

He started to shake and swore again, reaching forward to knock the heat up another notch. He was cold, wet, and angry. He was feeling things he didn't want to feel, and Cheyenne was too damn far away to suit him.

She could have helped, for a while anyway, but she didn't want to. She was showing more sense than he, he was sure.

He had her home in under five minutes of strained silence, pulling up in front of the white picket fence surrounding her yard. She lived on the northeastern edge of town, on a dirt-and-gravel side street that wound down into muddy ruts across the Great Plains.

He was supposed to say something, but the

effort was beyond him. Not even a simple good-bye could get out of him without making him feel worse. She'd have to say it for both of them, then just open the door and leave. He couldn't say good-bye, not when he wanted her to turn to him and ask him to stay.

"You're freezing." The words came to him softly. "Shivering."

When, he wondered, had she gotten so dumb? She had to know better than to be kind.

He tilted his head to one side and stared right through her, right through to the heart of her. If she wasn't going to make it easy, he was going to make it damn hard, impossible if he could.

He saw a flicker of panic brighten her eyes. He saw a soft swallow slide down her throat. But she held her ground and managed to speak again.

"Why don't you come inside. I'll dry your shirt for you."

He accepted the invitation with silent actions, turning off the ignition and getting out.

He didn't know who was the bigger fool, her for asking him to stay, or him for accepting. Somebody was bound to get hurt, probably both of them. He didn't know if he was strong enough to stay if she had a lot of rules about it, but he did know he wasn't strong enough to leave.

He was a Navy lieutenant, a SEAL, a team leader, the quintessential definition of toughness and discipline. He knew about going the extra mile, or the extra ten, and his body was trained to give him what he needed without faltering. He made snap decisions, had done it under fire, sending men into places from which they hadn't come back—and she was laying him low. Even his body was caught up in her, racing to get closer and closer despite all his doubts.

He held the door open as she stepped inside, and she brushed against him, hip to thigh, the most fleeting of connections. His body tensed in instant reaction. If she had a lot of rules, they'd be broken before he left.

Sarah didn't know who was winning and who was losing. She had no idea what Colt was thinking, but she did know she wasn't ready to let him go. That seemed to be her bottom line. She wasn't proud of it.

"I'll make some coffee." The simple things were the best, she thought, and nothing was simpler than making a pot of coffee. When she actually got to the kitchen, though, the task took on new proportions of difficulty. She didn't know how many cups to make, a full pot or just a half. It depended on how long he was staying, and she didn't know that. Then there was the problem of how strong he liked it.

She stood at the counter with the filter holder in one hand and a spoonful of coffee in the other, stymied by the variables. She knew what was wrong. She was overwhelmed; her pulse was racing. She needed to calm down and sort things out, think and act like a regular person.

The sound of his footsteps instantly dispelled her hopes in that direction.

"I like it pretty strong." He offered the advice, and she acted on it, dumping several measures of coffee into the filter, enough for a full pot. When he left it wouldn't be because she'd run out of coffee.

She poured in the water and punched the button, which left her with nothing to do but turn around. She did, carefully, and caught him at a bad time anyway.

His shirt was draped over one of her kitchen chairs, but his T-shirt was in transition up his torso, with his face covered and his arms crossed over his head. He was California tan, his skin a silky, golden brown. The muscles in his chest and abdomen were sculpted with exquisite definition, the only flaw being a white line that ran from his right shoulder, across his chest, and down to the bottom of his rib cage on the left. She reached for him without thinking, a slight, shocked movement, but stopped herself in time to keep from trespassing.

Colt felt the near touch and the quick jerking away, and he knew what had caused both. He'd forgotten about the scars. He pulled his head out of the T-shirt and drew it off his arms. He handed it to her along with his shirt and watched her gather them to her breasts, billowing his clothing between her fingers.

"You've been hurt," she said softly, still staring at his chest.

"A few times."

"What happened?"

"I miscalculated. An enemy took me by surprise."

The look she gave him told him how strange she found his answer. Most people didn't live in a world where enemies committed physical violence on them, and he wouldn't be the one to tell her this particular act of violence had occurred in her world. His commander knew what had happened to him—there was damn little his commander didn't know about him—but the origin of the scar wrapping three quarters around his neck and the one cutting diagonally across his chest wasn't common knowledge, no more so than the parallel marks tracking across his back.

He'd been identified and catalogued in every possible way from the top of his head to the bottoms of his feet, and the scars were a part of his official record. But to Sarah they meant only pain. He saw it in her eyes.

"It wasn't as bad as it looks," he said in an attempt to reassure her and shift her attention. Bull hadn't carved his initials into his handiwork, but to Colt it had always been obvious what the scars were: the marks of a whip.

She didn't look convinced, but she turned away. "I'll get you something to wear while your clothes dry." To her credit, her voice didn't waver. It was terribly quiet, but it didn't waver.

He followed her into the living room, then waited while she continued on into the hall leading to the bedrooms and a bath. Her home was nice, he decided after looking around. The furniture wasn't new, but neither was it shabby. Everything was done up in light colors. There was a lot of soft whiteness—at the windows, in the couch pillows, woven through the oriental rug in the living room. It was a woman's place, Sarah's place, right where he wanted to be.

He shoved his hands in his pockets and hunched his shoulders. He was freezing. She'd turned on a couple of lamps, but he needed heat. He needed her—and so far, he'd stayed off his knees. He was grateful for the small victory, but it wasn't nearly enough.

Rain streaked the long windows on the south wall of her living room, the ones facing back toward town. He didn't think the storm was going to let up all night. Prairie storms were always intense, wildly beautiful if a person had the courage to face them. Geography gave them an edge: A man could see one coming from miles off, fill himself up with worry and anticipation, but when he was under it there wasn't a way out and nothing to stop it, no mountains and damn few trees.

He heard her coming back down the hall and turned to face her. She looked frightened and unsure, his wet shirts clutched to her chest with one hand and a football jersey hanging from the other. He couldn't help her, not as long as they stayed at a polite impasse, not if all they did was drink her coffee and sit on her couch while his clothes rose and fell in her dryer.

She offered him the jersey. When he took it, he wrapped his hand around both the shirt and her hand and drew her near. Her hesitation was real, and so were the doubts clouding her face, but she came.

Shirts wet and dry were bunched between them, until he took her hand and opened it over his chest. The jersey floated to the floor. The wet shirts followed when he grasped her other hand and slipped it around his waist. Her fingers were coolly damp as they slid across his skin.

Her breasts rose against him on a trembling breath, triggering an inevitable reaction deep inside his body. She probably wanted to talk first, he thought. It would be the sensible thing.

But sensibility wasn't a place he could reach just then. Passion was. Love and lust, sweet consummation, a driving coalescence of his desire were all effortlessly within his reach when he was within her arms.

They could talk later.

Five

Sarah knew he was going to kiss her, and she knew she was going to be undone. The die had been cast.

A painfully slow breath escaped her. His arm came around her waist, indomitable. His fingers caressed her cheek, feathering across her skin with a gentleness at odds with the strength of his hand.

"Colt . . . no." The words barely made it out of her mouth; their lack of conviction almost made them silent.

He kissed her anyway. His mouth brushed over hers, his tongue barely tasted her lips, but it was enough to start the heat inside, that quick flicker of wetness.

She didn't move—she couldn't—and after only a second's pause he kissed her again, tightening his arm around her in an act of possession. The descent of his darkly golden head was unerring. His tongue dampened her lips in one long, sure stroke of claiming. The gesture was forcibly male. He'd marked her as his, and she trembled inside.

He wanted her. He was going to take her, all the way, in every way. She remembered how it had been between them, and the memories and the building heat weakened her knees. She clung to him, her small hands pressed to his chest, feeling his muscles bunch and give with every move he made. No one felt like Colton Haines. No one had ever felt as good.

He angled his open mouth over hers, making the kiss deeper, more demanding, and infinitely sweeter and wetter. Breaths mingled. Tongues stroked and slid across each other. Whimpered sounds of distress and desire mixed with short, deep groans. He was seductive and single-minded, and Sarah was stripped of self-defense. He cupped her breast, filling his hand, and she was undone, completely undone.

"No . . ." She tore herself from his arms and turned her back to him, hiding her face in her hands. Her cheeks were hot. She shook her head and tried to control the trembling of her body. "Don't . . . don't do this."

Colt heard the plea in her voice, the edge of panic, but he didn't stop. She'd have to do better than that to dissuade him, when she was melting against him with every touch. He came up behind her and wrapped his arm around her hips, holding her close, pressing himself into the soft roundness of her bottom, molding himself to her and feeling the pleasure surge through his groin.

Sarah felt it, too, his hardening maleness. She felt his hand gather her hair from her neck and move it aside, and she felt his mouth come down on her nape, hot and wet, his tongue laying a trail of fire across her skin. The impact of his touch, the boldness, rocked her very soul.

She turned to face him, to reason with him or abandon herself to him, she didn't know which. He fit himself to her even more intimately, and for a long, intense moment her breath wouldn't come, let alone words. His gaze held hers, fiercely intent, shot through with desire and his need for her, only her.

"No." A single word finally came, denying him. More words followed in a voice so soft, even she barely heard it. "We aren't what we were, Colt. We can't be. We're not kids anymore. We can't pick up where we left off. Life doesn't work that way."

"I don't want what we were. I want what we are." His voice was much steadier than hers, with plenty of conviction to back it up.

Sarah forced away a sudden sensation of defeat. He was stronger than she, stronger and smarter, and more realistic. For she still mourned what they'd had together. In the privacy of her loneliest nights she remembered what they'd been and she missed him. She'd missed him for ten years, well past the point of common sense, or reason, or reality. He'd become the unreachable dream, the unfulfilled fantasy. He wasn't ever supposed to have shown up in her living room wanting her, tempting her. Those wishes, those daydreams of a broken heart had died a long time ago. He wasn't supposed to have come back. It was too late, too damn late.

"We're nothing, Colt. That's what I'm telling

you," she said, willing her voice above the intimacy of a whisper. "You're a—a Navy officer in California, and I'm a pharmacist in Wyoming. There's no connection."

Except, she added silently, for the miles of emotion tangling around her heart and tying her to him. Except for the charge of desire she felt with every pulse beat, the jolt of her senses every time he touched her. Except for wanting him, and remembering him, and always and forever missing him, there was no connection.

She should be stronger.

A wry smile touched the corner of his mouth. "You're wrong. I'm still the same man I always was."

"You were a boy, just a boy," she insisted, looking away.

He cupped her chin with his hand, and against her will she obeyed the silent command and met his gaze.

Lamplight shone along the lean, hardened planes of his face. His voice grew quiet and serious, like the azure-fired depths of his eyes. "I wasn't a boy that night with you, Sarah, and never again afterward."

Something in his words hurt her, as if she had stolen something from him.

"I wasn't the one who left," she instinctively said in her defense.

"You weren't the one who couldn't stay."

Unheralded, thunder crashed against the sky in a flash of blinding light, startling her and sending her deeper into his arms. The lights in the house flickered, then died, and they were left in the graying darkness of an overcast twilight. His hands tightened on her.

"Whatever else you're thinking," he said, "you have to know we're right together. Can't you feel it?"

She felt it, and it scared her senseless, but she said nothing.

"I feel it." He spoke low, his voice taking on the edge of a plea. "I feel it right down through the center of everything I am, and I've only felt this way with you. That *has* to mean something."

A long time ago she'd called what he was feeling "love," but she wouldn't make a fool out of herself by throwing that powerful word into the conversation. Love was impossible.

"I'm not saying things are the same. They're not. I remember—" He broke off and swore softly, his hands tightening on her again. Glancing down for a second, he took a breath, then faced her again. "I never forgot, Sarah. I never forgot anything. I remember how you came to me, how you touched me. I remember how you surprised me." For an instant a smile creased his cheek, a flash of mischief warmed his eyes. "Lord, how you surprised me."

Her face burned. She knew what he was talking about, and she thought it was terribly impolite of him to mention their past intimacies. Impolite and alarmingly exciting, those memories of what she'd done to him, how and where she'd kissed him, and what had happened after the kissing.

"Things—things are different now," she stammered, wishing there was someplace to look besides his chest, or his bare, sleekly muscled belly, or the stretched material at the front of his pants.

"Things are different," he agreed. She felt his breath in her hair, his mouth on her brow. "But you're still going to know I'm the man on you, the man inside you . . . taking you over the edge."

Yes. She answered him with a silent, near-physical yearning. She knew he spoke the truth, and he made the truth sound like heaven.

A whisper of cool air on her skin warned her of what he was doing to the buttons down the front of her dress. His mouth roamed over her face, kissing, licking, gently grazing her with his teeth, actions that had immediate effects up and down her body. Not a word of protest could get beyond any one of those effects. He was kissing her and undressing her, and nothing else mattered. No amount of sense and rationality could hold back the wave rolling over her. She needed to feel him, his hands on her, his body, hard and male, sliding against hers. Abandonment it would be, heaven.

Colt sensed the tension leaving her body, and sensed pliancy and submission take its place. For all his need of her, he felt a predatory satisfaction in winning her once again, in making her his.

He pushed her dress over her shoulders and down her arms, letting it slide to the floor with a rustling caress. He caught sight of a pink slip trimmed in beige lace, the tiny satin straps rounded against the flat white elastic straps of her bra. Both were so very feminine. Both were pushed aside.

Her reaction was instinctive—she caught the lingerie before it fell away and revealed her breasts. He didn't mind. She was softly female in his arms, the most beautiful woman he'd ever seen, ever held. The crush of her slip against his chest entranced him. Her fragrance surrounded him, fascinating. He ran his mouth down her throat, across her collarbone, tasting and tracing the lines of her body. By the time he reached her breast she was completely his. His name sighed from her lips as she clung to him, letting her clothing fall where it may, reveal what it might.

His world started coming together, pieces fitting into slots, gears meshing. She'd always been good, so easy, so easy to make good love with. Her responses were genuine, hotly erotic—like the way she lifted her hips against him—and nothing helped him more. He drew her breast deeper into his mouth. God, she was sweet, so utterly female.

He slid his hands up her thighs and beneath her slip, then worked down her underthings till the hosiery and panties pooled around her ankles. He slipped them off her feet and rose in front of her, his hands sliding over softer, more giving curves, over satiny skin and soft lingerie.

He liked taking her clothes off. He liked it the way he liked breathing. He liked rediscovering what he'd worked so hard to forget.

Her hair still reached her breasts, straight and silky, so artless, so feminine, so Sarah. With the tiny straps hanging loose on her arms and her hair tangling over her shoulders, she looked unbound, willing.

He kissed her mouth, running his tongue over teeth, remembering all the times he'd held himself in check when they'd been younger, remembering the day he hadn't and how intense their lovemaking had been. She moved against him, and he automatically returned the favor, and pressing her back against the wall, kissing her harder, pushing her for more.

He knew what he wanted and he knew how to get it. He'd been trained to conquer, and tonight she was his purpose, his ambition. He bunched her slip in his hand and drew it up over her hips, holding it at the small of her back as he slipped his other hand down her body, his fingers sliding into moist, soft folds, into mystery. She moaned into his mouth, starting an avalanche of sensation and arousal he wanted to drown in.

Whispering half-formed thoughts, incoherent urgings, she moved against his hand, then turned the tables on him, reaching down to free him from his pants. She worked at his button, his zipper, his underwear, half inept, and he let her fumble. He let the anticipation lift him to a fever pitch, until she shoved his clothing off his hips. Then he was the one being conquered, the one being taken. She stroked him and stole his breath, telling him she remembered too—how to please him, how to make him hers.

"Sarah . . ." He groaned her name, his arm tightening around her, as if he was afraid she might try to leave him, release him, when what he wanted was to be captured completely. He hadn't forced himself on her just for something quick, easy, and empty. He needed her clinging to him, coming apart in his arms, all over him. He needed her weak with fulfillment to make him strong.

He kissed her eyelids and her cheeks, and the corners of her mouth, indulging himself in her pleasure, emotionally sinking into her. Pushing against her, he measured himself against her readiness, waiting for her to want him. When she did, it was sweet death—the passion of her mouth on his, her hand guiding him to the source of her heat, and her taking him in.

He swore, none too gently, and apologized, but he kept pushing into her, withdrawing a ways, then coming on again and sliding deeper, hitting a rhythm of the purest physical pleasure. His world narrowed down to the joining of their bodies and the joining of their mouths, to the slick friction of taking her and loving her.

Warm currents raced and pulsed through Sarah's veins, converging in private places like cascading pools, each more sublime than the last, magnetic and fluid, a lodestone for the driving, tumid length of him. Their kiss was wild, crazily out of control. When he shifted his hold on her, lifting her higher to meet his thrusts, the rest of the world followed the wildness. She gasped his name.

Colt needed no more stimulus, no more incentive than her first sweet contraction to trigger his own release. He sank into her, his body going rigid as the first shudder ripped through him and the others followed, all of it rolling over him and back on itself, endlessly. Timeless catharsis. He'd wanted her. He'd wanted her so very badly. Just this . . . only this.

Sarah was limp, completely wrung out, and held on to Colt for dear life. His muscles quivered, and his breath was heavy and ragged in the crook of her neck. She didn't know how he stayed on his feet, for hers wouldn't hold her, not yet. She needed him for support, and his body stayed warm, and hard, and reliable, firmly there despite all the latent remains of passion racing under his skin.

A totally irreverent thought crossed her mind: Maybe once every ten years was enough of this sort of thing. A person wouldn't last long doing it every day.

She'd been engaged once, to a man she'd dated for over a year, and in comparison to what had just happened between Colt and her, she and her fiancé had barely managed the most casual of sexual relations.

Colt was not casual, never had been, not when it came to her. She could take it for one night, though. She dipped her head and kissed his neck, stealing a taste with her tongue. He was salty with sweat, hot, wonderfully male, and probably addicting. The important thing was not to fall in love.

"Did I hurt you?" His grip on her relaxed, letting her slide down the length of him to the floor. A mistake, judging by the quick hiss of his indrawn breath and his muttered curse.

"Did I hurt *you*?" she asked.

"No." He lifted his head from her shoulder and recaptured her mouth once, fiercely. "But I'll give you another chance at it."

And so it went, on into the night. He took everything she had and more than she'd thought possible to give. In return he poured all of himself into her, filling her with more than her fantasies had imagined, more passion than she thought she could bear, more love and sadness than she could absorb.

She knew she was being used. Of that she had no doubts. But the time for saying no to him had been in the church basement, and he was so tender, so painfully honest. He'd made no promises to get into her bed. He'd hardly spoken at all.

He hadn't needed to, she admitted on a quiet sigh, pulling her quilt up higher on his shoulder. She hoped she didn't do anything ridiculous, like never wash her sheets again, but he smelled so good. Not good in the traditional sense, like rain-washed forests, or baking bread. His scent was more animal, muskier, deep and comforting, especially when she was drifting off to sleep half in his arms, just breathing him in.

He was asleep now. She'd awakened only moments before, still thinking the same thoughts she'd had throughout the evening—or, in truth, since his mother's death. She'd known Amanda's son would come home. The rest of it had been a mystery, but he was there in her bed, and dawn was only a couple of hours away.

He was so beautiful. Moonlight shone along his hair and the hard curves of his arm, down to his broad hand lying open on the patchwork quilt. His face held a look of concentration, but his breathing was even. He'd woken once with a jerk and a gasped cry. She'd held him and talked to him, reassured him she was there. Then she'd kissed him on the cheek, like a mother with a child, and he'd responded soundlessly, like a lover, rolling her over and covering her with his body.

The trick, she reminded herself now, the important thing was to not make a fool of herself when he left in the morning. Surely she could drag together enough pride to get through a clean good-bye. She must have a whole storehouse of unused pride locked up somewhere inside herself.

She closed her eyes and inhaled the scent of warm, love-sated man. In the morning she was going to wish she'd been stronger.

But tonight . . . tonight she was sleeping with Colton Haines.

Six

Sarah had been right. She woke up alone, and with a quick, stabbing pain she wished she'd been stronger. The breath she forced herself to take did not have the desired calming effect. Instead, it tingled all the way up her nose and pushed the waiting tears nearer to the surface.

Her bedroom blurred into a watery vision of flowered wallpaper and maple furniture. The draped curtains at the windows masked the brightness of the day, but the quality of light told her it was well past dawn. He'd probably been gone for hours. She wondered if he'd thought about waking her, or if he'd been glad to get away unnoticed and dry of any tears she might have shed.

She was nobody's fool, not even Colton Haines's, but one-night stands were a bit beyond her experience. And he—damn him—he'd given her two, her *only* two. She wanted to strangle him for leaving her without a word. She wanted to hit him hard, knock some sense into him. But all she had was the pillow he'd slept on, and all she could do was wrap her arms around it and cry all over it, cursing him for leaving her. She knew how to hurt and hate and love at the same time. He'd taught her all about it a long time ago.

If sex had any power whatsoever as an antidote to grief, then she hoped he felt better. She hoped he was on his way to California feeling a whole lot better than when he'd blown back into her life like a wild summer storm.

She felt worse.

Damn him. Damn him. Damn him. She was a woman, not a girl, and she was supposed to know better than to get herself hurt. She'd ridiculously underestimated his potential effect on her emotions, though. Fool.

A ragged sob burst free, getting past her willpower and her anger. She clutched his pillow tighter, buried her face deeper, and that made everything worse. The scent that had been so comforting when he was sleeping next to her was torture when she was alone. She'd be washing her sheets all right, just as soon as she got herself out of bed.

He was the one who had talked about feeling something right every time he saw her. Which he'd made a grand effort to do once this decade, she reminded herself. She'd said no such thing—but, Lord, how she'd felt it.

She groaned and rolled over onto her back, pulling his pillow on top of her chest. Shameless. No other word described what she'd done, what she'd allowed to happen, inviting him inside like that. Yes, he'd been shivering, but he could have shivered himself back to the Regent Motel and she'd have been none the worse.

Her tears welled up, spilling onto her cheeks. What a terrible liar she was. She no more could have sent him to the motel to grieve alone than she could truly hate him. She had high hopes of maturing beyond being in thrall to a pathetically one-sided infatuation, but until that happened she wasn't going to beat herself over the head for taking what he'd offered.

As a lover he was passionate, overwhelmingly so, and mostly tender, but rough in ways that had at times left her breathless. She hadn't been loved as well since . . . since the last time they'd lain together.

And he hadn't lied. She would always give him that, even though it put her in a less than saintly light. She'd known when he'd first kissed her in the church what he'd wanted. He'd wanted her, and a true and redeeming pleasure had blossomed inside her at the knowledge, a pride that went beyond appearance and accomplishments to a purer essence. Colton Haines had still wanted her, after all the years, all the changes. He'd still wanted her—for one lousy, glorious night.

She slugged his pillow, grunting with the power of her punch, giving the down a good uppercut.

"Ouch," another voice answered, and she froze with her fist buried in fluff.

"I guess that's for me," his softly modulated Wyoming drawl teased her from across the bedroom. "Unless you always wrestle with the bedclothes in the morning."

She peeked over the edge of the pillow for confirmation of his presence before squeezing her eyes shut and sinking back into the bed. He hadn't left her. He was standing in her doorway, filling it up with his hard, muscled body, dressed in a pair of jeans and a dark western-cut shirt.

"I have coffee," he said, and with a start of alarm she realized he was coming closer.

She popped her head above the pillow, wiping hastily at her cheeks. "Thank you," she said, hoping to hold him off. "I'll be out in just a minute." The last word left her on a squeak as he sat down on the bed, very close indeed.

"You've been crying." One eyebrow lifted in confusion, then a dawning understanding flickered in his eyes. "Is that for me too?"

Given half a chance, she thought irritably, he would leave her with nothing, not even a scrap of decorum to hide behind. The man asked for too much and got most of what he asked for, but she was drawing the line at verbal admissions.

"I'd like some privacy, please."

For a moment she thought he wasn't going to comply with her request. His gaze held hers steadily, searching her with an intensity she found disturbing and—dammit—exciting. She tightened her hold on his pillow.

Colt caught the small movement and backed off. He wasn't sure what else to do. He felt a lot of things, most of them conflicting, especially when it came to her. He wanted to crawl back into bed with her and start all over again, but what rationality he'd regained in the light of day told him that was sure emotional suicide. The same rationality had told him to leave earlier, when he'd first wakened. He'd been tempted. It had seemed such a neat, clean way to part. But the United States

Navy hadn't trained him to be a coward, and his mother hadn't raised him to be cruel.

He would have had to have been both to have walked away from her while she slept—and a good deal less self-indulgent besides. She was exquisite in sleep, her mouth swollen from his kisses, her golden lashes like sunbursts on her cheeks. He'd marked her all over, from where his beard had left chafed marks on her neck and on the curves of her breasts, to the tiny bites on her thighs. He hadn't meant to use her so hard. But her skin had an overall glow, and he knew he'd given her that too.

Her eyes were turning warier by the second, and remembering he was a gentleman, he pushed off her bed and left the room. It would have been easier, for him anyway, to take his clothes off and slip between the sheets and her legs. Easier, known, and definitely enjoyable. Meeting her in the kitchen for coffee was none of the above.

Sarah took her time. She showered, shampooed, and blow-dried, and in between times she kept an ear cocked for any sounds of his leaving. She changed her pants twice and her shirt three times, buttoning and unbuttoning while she roamed from closet to window, drawing the curtains aside for quick glances at the street and his jeep. The Sunday morning sky was deteriorating almost as fast as her courage. There would be a fresh storm soon.

Red was a good color on her; so was white. She chose blue, powder blue. The shirt was pure cotton, collarless, and had at least twenty finger-defying buttons down the front. Jeans were jeans, but she picked her "fat" jeans, and she was in one of her skinny periods. The material bunched around her waist, especially when cinched with a belt. The silver-tipped end of the belt hung down a ways, giving her what her best friend, Ellen Calhoun, Daniel's wife, had assured her was a loose, sexy sort of look.

She dragged a brush through her hair in front of her bureau mirror, frowning at her loose, sexy sort of look. That was the world she lived in, a place where her best friend had to let her know when she looked attractive, or sexy, because no one else either cared enough to notice or felt beholden to let her know.

Colt had noticed, and he'd certainly let her know.

She was crazy to go out there looking loose and sexy.

Estrangement and death have a few things in common: the cessation of contact, the slow evolution of life without the other person, until all the places that person filled have been filled by something else, at least on the surface. The deeper places are never filled.

Colt doubted if he'd written his mother three times the first year he'd been gone, or twice the second year. The third year he didn't write at all, but he'd called her from Tokyo once and talked up half his pay. By his fourth year out of Wyoming he was a different man from the one who'd left. He'd been under fire and he'd seen men die, one of them cradled in his lap with his blood making the concrete floor slick beneath their boots. Colt remembered yelling for help, and he remembered the next round coming in. There had been an explosion and a fire, and more gunshots, yet through it all, he'd known exactly when Max had died, exactly at what point the life in his arms had ceased to exist.

He'd called his mother more often after that.

Nothing in life is easy, especially the leaving of it, especially for the ones who are left.

He leaned on the kitchen counter, his arms stiff, his mouth tight as he stared out the window, not knowing exactly which way to run to get away from the hurt. He'd cried the day they'd told him, and he'd be damned if he knew why women claimed it made them feel better. It had made him feel like hell. He hoped not to do it again.

Sarah had been crying for him that morning, and he didn't know what to do about that either. He didn't know what to do about her, about what they'd done and how she made him feel.

He lowered his head and stretched the muscles across his shoulders. God knows, he'd never met anyone else like her. She was a comfort, and he didn't mean anything simple or passive. Within her body she held the power of life, like a river flowing. She was heat on a frozen day, food in an empty belly, a place to be—but not without a price.

She entered the kitchen behind him, and he pushed his thoughts aside, forcing himself to relax. He turned with as much smile as he could muster, knowing she deserved more.

"I saved you some bacon and hash browns in the oven," he said. "I would have waited for you to get up, but I couldn't—too hungry." He also could have gone out for breakfast, but he hadn't trusted himself to come back. "Can I fix you an egg? There's one left."

He'd thought about that, too, making himself at home in her kitchen and cooking her food, and decided it was the best thing to do. After the way he'd invaded her home and her bed—and her— drawing the line at her kitchen would have been a slap in the face, as if her body and her bedroom were less important than her cupboards and re- frigerator. He hadn't wanted to remind her that in many ways they were practically strangers. So he'd made himself at home and cooked up all her bacon and all but one of her eggs, even though he wasn't at all sure he'd be there long enough to take her out for lunch to even the score.

Even the score. Lord, what a rotten thing to think.

"Sure," she answered him. "I like mine scram- bled." She poured herself a cup of coffee and got the milk out of the refrigerator, moving around the kitchen with an easy, natural grace, while he was glued to the counter, measuring every word for fear of offending her or hurting her feelings.

He cracked the egg into a bowl he'd had ready by the stove. Months of shared Saturday morning breakfasts at the Rock Creek Cafe had earned them a permanently reserved booth by the win- dow. He hadn't forgotten how she liked her eggs. He should have, but he hadn't.

Sarah liked watching him cook. She liked mak- ing him nervous as a cat. After the way he'd steamrolled her, it was a refreshing novelty. He'd been in charge in the bedroom, but she obviously had the upper hand in the kitchen.

"When are you leaving?" she asked.

The bowl clattered to the counter and he swore under his breath. She waited as he got it all back together again and finally answered.

"Today."

"They didn't give you much time, did they?" she managed to say after a small eternity.

"I didn't ask for much."

"Oh." She sipped her coffee.

"Ruby's taking care of everything," he added when an explanation seemed required.

Ruby had been Amanda's partner in the beauty shop and her best friend. She was probably far more familiar with the details of Amanda's day-to-day life than Colton. Given the state of the town's economy, Sarah doubted if there were any assets that needed protecting, other than the ranch where Amanda's trailer was set up, where Colt had at one time run a small herd.

"The land is mine," he said, answering her unspoken thoughts. "Has been for years. The way business was, she wanted to make sure nobody could get at it, so she gave it to me." He turned and set her breakfast on the table.

"Looks great," she said, keeping her tone light despite the nearly suffocating weight in her chest.

He didn't move, but continued standing next to her chair, until she became uncomfortably aware of the worn softness of his jeans and the body underneath, the curves of his thighs and the pale creases in the denim covering him. Her gaze lowered to his boots, fairly new and stitched in an intricate pattern. She noted the way one knee lifted fractionally higher than the other when he shifted his weight. In a few long, slow seconds, she found herself back at his waist, having visually cruised the length of his legs from boot to buckle. She blushed at the realization.

"Thank you," she said, clearing her throat and picking up her fork. "For breakfast." He still didn't move.

"Thank *you*, Sarah. Thank you for everything." His voice was soft and ragged.

Her blush deepened.

Colt knew his words were inadequate, that they weren't quite right, and it created a sense of frustration inside him. He wanted to thank her and apologize to her, and somehow let her know what being with her had meant. But he didn't know where to start and he wasn't sure if stumbling over and around the subject would make things better or worse. Her silence had him wishing he'd made it easier on both of them and just left.

Over the years he'd slept with a few women he probably shouldn't have, spent nights where he hadn't belonged. But there had been so little for him with those women, the leaving had never been more than slightly embarrassing.

Sarah was tearing his heart out. He'd loved her too much a long time ago to treat her differently now, yet the circumstances were so very different. Knowing his limits was what kept him alive, and he'd badly miscalculated last night.

"Colt, sit down, please," she said, barely meeting his eyes, her fingers fidgeting with her fork.

He should have gotten back in bed with her, he thought. He'd known it from the moment he'd left her alone in the bedroom. If he had, they'd be doing something they'd both shown a good, solid aptitude for. Instead they were pushing off into uncharted territory. He felt naked and unprepared.

"Please," she repeated.

He sat down, and just as quickly got back up to retrieve his coffee cup from the counter. Then he sat down again and waited, and as he waited his knee started to sway back and forth, his foot rocking on the slant heel of his boot. His mind started to hum *Cheyenne . . . Cheyenne . . . Cheyenne.*

She was making a coward out of him, plain and simple. She could have been the enemy's secret weapon. Forget espionage and terrorism, forget hostages and misinformation. Sarah Brooks had his number.

"Colt . . ." she began, her head lowered, her gaze on her untouched egg. "I don't know what you think happened last night, but—"

It was worse than he'd thought. They were going to dissect the night. His hands tightened around his cup, and his knee went from a sway to a jiggle.

"—I want you to know everything is okay."

And?

"You didn't hurt me, and you certainly didn't make me do anything I didn't want to do."

His knee came to a slow stop. She didn't know how to play the game very well. No killer instinct.

He stared at the top of her head, then followed the slope of her nose down to her still-swollen mouth, and his gut tightened. No, no killer instinct there, not a whit. Her lips were sweet and vulnerable, the flush on her cheeks disarming. He reached across the table and slid his hand around hers, pulling her near enough to entwine their fingers.

She said he hadn't hurt her. He didn't believe her for a minute, but he would let her have things her way. She knew best.

Her skin was soft beneath his caressing thumb, her bones delicate, and he was such a bastard. She knew best how to ease his guilt. And knew best how to let him go.

He'd done his duty. He had stayed to say good-bye. Now it was time to walk away.

Seven

Some parts of Wyoming were so godforsaken, Colt doubted if more than a couple people even knew they existed. His current position was the perfect example: forty miles outside of Rock Creek, somewhere between Cheyenne and the edge of nowhere. He'd never seen so damn much empty highway.

He'd shaken her hand when he'd left. He still couldn't believe it. He'd kissed her, too, on the cheek, but their last contact had been him shaking her hand.

It would be good to get back to Coronado, where he knew what was going on and how to handle himself. Maybe he'd tell Garrett what had happened. Garrett was his second in command. They'd been through a lot together, including most of Europe and half of the Middle East.

He shifted uneasily in his seat. No, he wouldn't be talking to Garrett about Sarah. If he told Garrett the truth, he knew one sailor who would be taking his next leave in Rock Creek, and unlike himself, Garrett was real smooth with women.

The miles wore away beneath the wheels of his military jeep, and the rain poured down on the semi-arid land that rolled to the ends of the earth all around him. He had a plane to catch in Cheyenne.

He swore and whacked the steering wheel with his open palm. He couldn't believe he'd shaken her hand.

Sundays were the longest day of the week, and this one was stacking up to be more endless than most. Sarah had washed the breakfast dishes, tidied up the living room, and scrubbed the kitchen floor, but she hadn't washed her sheets. She hadn't had time really, she told herself. Also, she'd just changed the bed on Saturday, so it seemed a shame to do it again so quickly, a waste of water and energy and all that.

He'd shaken her hand. She didn't know what that meant. Probably nothing, just like the whole damn night meant nothing to him.

She pushed herself out of her armchair and wandered over to the living room windows. The sky was dark and rolling, full of lightning and thunder. Rain beat against her front porch and ran in rivulets down the chains of the swing. He shouldn't have made love to her in the living room. It made it too hard to get away from him. Maybe she'd go to Sunday evening service at church.

Oh, right. Church. That's the perfect place to get away from him. She made a face at her reflection in the window. What an idiot you are, she thought, and gave the wall a scuffing kick.

Great, now she had something to keep her busy. Another mindless cleaning project.

"Yes, sir . . . No, sir . . . Aye, sir." Colt squeezed tighter into the pay phone, hunching his shoulders and flipping up the collar on his jacket. The rain was coming down in sheets a few inches behind him, running off the eaves of the gas station, the only thing in Oates, Wyoming, population two hundred and four—an exaggeration if he'd ever seen one.

He'd stopped for gas and started thinking, or maybe he'd started thinking and stopped for gas. Either way, he hadn't called his commanding officer for the sole purpose of getting chewed out, however benignly. He wanted more time. He was getting it, but not without the lecture.

"Aye, sir, and thanks, skipper." One week, and he could keep the jeep, compliments of Warren Air Force Base in Cheyenne. Some strings were going to get pulled there, that was for damn sure.

He hung up the phone and lowered his head to rest it against the receiver. He was going back to Rock Creek. He hoped to hell he could figure out why before he got there.

Sunday evening service was a solace. The church was quiet, more than half empty. The sermon was encouraging, and the friends and neighbors she talked with were more kind than curious, though Sarah realized that everyone in a ten-mile radius knew Colton Haines had spent the night at her house.

Every rule had an exception, though, and hers was Ellen, whose curiosity shone bright and clear, along with the kindness of her intentions.

"Are you okay?" her friend asked as they left the church together, Ellen's arm through hers, her head bending low and close.

If Sarah needed support, she knew it was there for the asking. She could talk her head off, or cry her eyes out, and Ellen Calhoun would take it all in, uncondemning.

She didn't want to talk, though, and she'd sworn not to cry.

"I'm doing pretty good," she said, giving her friend's arm a comforting squeeze.

Ellen was a rarity in Rock Creek, being neither born nor bred in the small town. Dark-haired, blue-eyed, and Southern, and well aware of all her other feminine assets, she was also the most self-assured woman ever to cross the threshold of Atlas Drugs. Daniel had met her in Denver at the Stock Show a few years back and married her within a week.

"And how's Colt?" Ellen asked, her drawl softening his name until it sounded like something warm to slip into, rather than a man who had walked out on Sarah without making even the pretense of ever returning. A man who had shaken her hand at the door.

Sarah stopped. Maybe she needed to talk after all.

Three cups of Rock Creek Cafe coffee later—coffee laced with the owner's private supply of brandy and topped with heavy dollops of whipped cream—Sarah wasn't nearly as concerned about the handshake as she had been.

"I shouldn't have taken him home, and that's all there is to it," she said, her voice higher than normal, her hands fluttering in little gestures of impatience.

"Don't you just hate hindsight?" Ellen turned to include the cafe's owner, who was behind the counter. "Don't you, Karla? Just hate hindsight?" In Ellen's mouth, the word "hindsight" had three syllables and "hate" had at least two, especially after brandy, but the older woman nodded in perfect understanding.

"Hindsight and men," Karla agreed. "Now there's a perfect pair."

"Or a roy'l flush," Ellen added, her eyes lighting up with mischief and mirth.

Sarah hiccuped in the middle of a short laugh. Karla chuckled as she went back to cleaning coffeepots.

"Guess we better get going," Ellen said. "Danny's going to send out a posse if I'm not home by eight-thirty."

The two women gathered up their purses and coats, and Sarah and Karla made quick plans for the next meeting of the Rock Creek Independent Businesswomen's Association. Sarah was the secretary and treasurer. Karla was the president and hospitality chairman, since they mostly met at the cafe. Amanda Haines had been the vice president. In a small town, losing one person left a lot of emptiness.

The cafe was only a block and a half from Sarah's house, but Ellen insisted on dropping her off and making sure she was okay. The latter

IT'S EASY TO ENTER THE WINNERS CLASSIC SWEEPSTAKES!
PRESENTED BY LOVESWEPT

Where will Passion lead you?

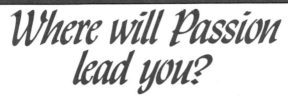

CARIBBEAN   EUROPE   HAWAII

YOU'RE INVITED

to enter our Winners Classic Sweepstakes presented by Loveswept for a chance to win a romantic 14-day vacation for two to Hawaii, Europe or the Caribbean ...PLUS $5,000 CASH!

Don't break our heart!

FREE ENTRY!   FREE BOOKS!

Peel off both halves of this heart and unite them on the Entry Form enclosed. Use both halves to get the most from this special offer.

SPECIAL BONUS:

Get 6 FREE Loveswept books, *plus* another wonderful gift just for trying Loveswept Romances. See details inside...

WIN THE ROMANTIC VACATION OF A LIFETIME...
PLUS $5000 SPENDING MONEY!

Take your pick — Hawaii, Europe or the Caribbean — and enjoy 14 passion-filled days and sultry nights if you're the winner of the Winners Classic Sweepstakes presented by Loveswept. It's *free* to enter, so don't miss out!

YOU COULD WIN YOUR DREAM TRIP!

Just peel off the FREE ENTRY side of our bright red heart, and place it on the Entry Form to the right. But don't stop there!

...AND GET LOVESWEPT EVERY MONTH!

Use the FREE BOOKS sticker and you'll get your first shipment of 6 Loveswept Romance books absolutely free! PLUS, we'll sign you up for the most romantic book service in the world! About once a month you get 6 new Loveswept novels. You always get 15 days to examine the books, and if you decide to keep them, you'll get 6 books for the price of 5! Be the first to thrill to these new stories. Your Loveswept books will always arrive before they're available in any store. There's no minimum. You can cancel at anytime by simply writing "cancel" on your invoice and returning the books to us. We'll pay the postage. So try the Loveswept romantic book service today!

Get a FREE lighted makeup case and 6 free Loveswept books!

Open the tortoise-shell finish case and the mirror lights up! Comes with a choice of brushes for lips, eyes and cheek blusher.

BOTH GIFTS ARE YOURS TO KEEP NO MATTER WHAT!

DON'T HOLD BACK!

1. No obligation! No purchase necessary! Enter our Sweepstakes for a chance to win!
2. FREE! Get your first shipment of 6 Loveswept books *and* a lighted makeup case as a free gift.
3. Save money! Become a member and about once a month you get 6 books for the price of 5! Return any shipment you don't want.
4. Be the first! You'll always receive your Loveswept books before they are available in stores. You'll be the first to thrill to these exciting new stories.

Detach here and mail today.

WINNERS CLASSIC SWEEPSTAKES
Entry Form

YES! I want to see where passion will lead me!

Place FREE ENTRY Sticker Here

Place FREE BOOKS Sticker Here

Enter me in the sweepstakes! I have placed my FREE ENTRY sticker on the heart.

Send me six *free* Loveswept novels *and* my *free* lighted makeup case! I have placed my FREE BOOKS sticker on the heart.

Mend a broken heart. Use both stickers to get the most from this special offer!

61234

NAME_____

ADDRESS_____ APT._____

CITY_____

STATE_____ ZIP_____

Loveswept's Heartfelt Promise to You!

There's no purchase necessary to enter the sweepstakes. There is no obligation to buy when you send for your free books and lighted makeup case. You may preview each new shipment for 15 days free. If you decide against it, simply return the shipment within 15 days and owe nothing. If you keep them, pay only $2.25 per book — a savings of 54¢ per book (plus postage, handling, and sales tax in NY and Canada.)

Prices subject to change. Orders subject to approval.

See complete sweepstakes rules at the back of this book.   LS1

Give in to love and see where passion leads you!
Enter the Winners Classic Sweepstakes and
send for your FREE lighted makeup case and
6 FREE Loveswept books today!

(See details inside.)

Detach here and mail today.

BUSINESS REPLY MAIL

FIRST-CLASS MAIL   PERMIT NO. 2456   HICKSVILLE, NY

POSTAGE WILL BE PAID BY ADDRESSEE

Loveswept

Bantam Doubleday Dell Direct, Inc.

P.O. Box 985

Hicksville, NY 11802-9827

NO POSTAGE
NECESSARY
IF MAILED
IN THE
UNITED STATES

proved either unnecessary or imperative or impossible, depending on a person's point of view. For when they rounded the corner, the first thing they both noticed was the military jeep parked in front of Sarah's white picket fence.

"Oh, my," Ellen breathed, stepping on the brake and stopping behind the jeep. They both looked toward Sarah's porch and saw his shadowy figure sitting in her swing.

Sarah was speechless.

"Put him on the couch, honey," Ellen said, "for your own peace of mind. Do you want me to have Danny call him?"

"No." The mere notion of involving another man in her situation, even a nice man like Daniel Calhoun, was enough to jump-start her voice. Men did things so differently from women. They were thoroughly unpredictable. "I'll be fine. I promise. The couch is a good idea. Colt and I can talk there." It all sounded so reasonable, but her heart was racing with a heady mixture of adrenaline, anticipation, and brandy. She was scared to expect too much, but she'd be damned if she'd accept too little.

He'd shown up on her doorstep, though, and that had to mean something.

Colt stood up the instant he saw the car. His first thoughts weren't good. Just because she hadn't mentioned a man by name the night before didn't mean she wasn't seeing someone. He steeled himself for the worst, knowing he was going to have a hard time if a man got out of the car with her.

No one got out of the car with her. The sedan pulled away as soon as Sarah shut the door, and

Colt discovered he liked that even less. If he was heading down a dead-end street, the sooner he figured it out the better. He wasn't proud of what he'd done. He'd played on her emotions, her memories, her tenderness. She'd always been sweet, and he'd gotten too coldhearted over the years. In his work, winning equated to surviving. Winners lived, and more often than not losers died. He'd won last night, and she'd let him win again this morning. He couldn't help but think she deserved better than some ruthless son of a bitch who'd left marks on her.

But he'd come back. Knowing all of it, he'd come back.

The gate swung shut behind her, snapping into the latch with the muted clank of metal against metal. The moon lit a path in the pools of rain left on her sidewalk. The storm had blown itself up into Nebraska and South Dakota, leaving the southeast corner of Wyoming floating in mud and ready to bloom.

"Colt." She spoke his name with an edge, a cool greeting.

He smiled in the dark. Anger he could handle. Challenges were always welcome.

"Sarah."

She mounted the steps to the porch and walked straight past him to the front door. Keys jingled in her hands for a minute or more before Colt realized she was having trouble. He watched her carefully, noting her awkwardness. Then she started to hum, tunelessly and under her breath. She kept trying keys, unperturbed by her lack of success. She wasn't angry. She was drunk.

"Can I help you?" he asked.

"No. Thank you." Her voice was curt.

So, she was angry with him after all, he thought, angry and drunk. Perfect.

He shifted his weight and ran his hand through his hair. He deserved this.

"What happened to your friend?" he asked.

"What friend?"

"The one who brought you home, but didn't wait to see if you got inside safely. The one who got you drunk."

Her reaction was to gasp and whirl around on him. "Ellen did most certainly not ever get me drunk! What a terrible thing to say!"

Ellen. Better than perfect. He started to relax, but she wasn't through with him.

"We saw you up here, skulking around. She wanted to call all sorts of people, all sorts, but I told her I could handle you." She lifted her chin a degree and met his gaze. "And I *can* handle you, Colton Haines."

He believed her beyond a doubt.

"I wasn't skulking," he said.

"Hummph." She turned back to her key-rattling business.

"Let me—"

The door opened on a sudden whoosh, and she stumbled inside, leaving him alone on the porch—but not for long. He picked up his bag and followed her inside, where she was already issuing her "handling" orders.

"You can sleep there, *only* there," she said, waving her hand at the couch as she passed through the living room on her way to the kitchen. "And if you've got anything you want to say, you can come in here to say it. I'm a little drunk. I need something to eat."

He dropped his bag at the end of the couch. Pots and pans rattled and rolled as he heard her drop one and then another. He headed for the kitchen, and his heart stopped when he reached the doorway.

"What in the hell"—he skirted the table running—"do you think you're doing?" He grabbed her with one arm around the waist, holding her where she was perched on tiptoe on a wobbly chair, reaching into the uppermost cabinet.

She turned to look at him and blinked, one hand wrapped around a plastic bottle, the other up against her mouth. She swallowed whatever she was holding and coughed.

"Taking vitamins," she said. "They're supposed to help. I think."

"You keep your vitamins up there?"

"I'm not real good about taking them. They always end up in the least-used spot."

"Well, the next time you want something up there, ask me." His voice was still tight.

She slanted him a droll look. "Sure. Like you're going to be here to get things out of my cupboards for me."

He was trying real hard, and she was pushing back even harder.

He lifted her off the chair and absently noted that her breasts were even with his mouth. Then the thought wasn't absent at all. Her hands were on his shoulders as he lowered her to the floor without releasing her. His gaze kept focusing on her mouth, and his thoughts kept getting ahead of his sense. He really needed to get a grip on his hormones, or his emotions, or his . . . whatever.

He hadn't come back just to bed her again, and if he had any doubts about it, she didn't.

"No," she said, her voice soft but firm. "There won't be any of that."

"No?" He wasn't sure she knew what she was talking about. He was looking at a woman he'd kissed and caressed a thousand ways in the night. He didn't think he'd last too long without doing it again.

"No." She gave her head a slight shake, loosening tendrils of hair from her barrette. "Sex with you is too—too much."

"Sex?" That hurt. It shouldn't have, but it did, even if he was the one who had stupidly shaken her hand like a schoolboy. "I thought—" He stopped himself. Thinking was getting him in too deep. She was right. He wouldn't be there next week to take her vitamins off the top shelf for her.

She'd looked away, but was still within his arms, and he felt the breath she took. When she spoke, her voice was even softer. "Being that way with you leaves me helpless, Colt. It's not something I can bear too much of, the helplessness. I'm a single woman who runs her own business in a town that's dying. I can't afford to want you, especially on a temporary basis.

"I can offer you a place to stay," she continued. "I'll let you make my breakfast again, and if you stay long enough, I'll cook your supper. I'll go out to your mom's with you, help where I can. But I can't give you my whole life to use up until you decide to leave."

No wonder so many men died in war, Colt thought. They didn't have the survival instincts of women. Hers were tempered steel with a diamond edge. After a moment's worth of reluctance, he released her and took a step back.

"I've got a week," he said, "if you'll have me that long. I sure as hell won't last seven nights at the Regent." And he'd never even considered staying at his mom's trailer. It wasn't the one he'd grown up in; it was the one she'd shared on and off with Bull Brooks. Knowing how Sarah had felt about her father ten years ago, he doubted if the man had ever set foot in her home, which suited him fine.

"You're welcome to stay." She caught his eye for a moment before turning away.

He intercepted her as she moved toward the stove. "Let me cook tonight before you break something. You can make it up to me at breakfast."

"I open the drugstore at nine."

"I'm usually awake by dawn."

"I close at five, except on Saturdays. Then I close at noon."

"I'll have supper ready."

"Sometimes I have deliveries that keep me at the store late, especially on Mondays."

"Then I'll take you to the cafe."

The conversation drifted into an easy pattern while he made himself at home in her kitchen. He steamed vegetables and poached two thawed chicken breasts in white wine, and she called him "California boy." He just grinned and sliced an apple to put on their plates.

During dinner they swapped college stories. Sarah had gone straight through and gotten her pharmacist's license. Colt's education had been more haphazard, and he'd let the Navy pay for most of it. He had a good degree, something the Navy required and something saleable in the civilian world.

"Math?" She didn't believe him. He'd always been smart, but not brainy. She remembered the gung-ho math majors at the University of Wyoming, the guys with ink stains on their pockets and calculators full of hieroglyphs.

"Sure. It comes in real handy for figuring stuff."

"What kind of stuff?" She still wasn't sure if he was pulling her leg or not.

"Explosives. Time, distance, speed. Plotting positions. Navigation. Practical stuff."

"Oh."

"Then there's the philosophical stuff, like chaos, and how far away are the farthest stars, and where is the beginning?"

She was still stuck on explosives. She picked up her knife and cut off a piece of chicken. "I've thought about what you do, a lot. I guess I always figured as long as I didn't hear you were dead, then you were fine."

"I'm practically desk-bound now. I'm getting old."

She expressed her opinion of his statement with one succinct word. He laughed.

"It's true. The only way I'm going to get hurt is if my office chair slips out from under me. You don't have to worry."

She wasn't going to admit to doing that anyway, but she didn't have any problem with calling him a liar.

"You don't have the look of the perpetually desk-bound," she said.

"We train a lot."

"What else do you do?"

"Most of the rest of what I do is classified." He was serious, but there was a teasing glint in his eyes. "I'm real good at keeping secrets, if you've got any you want to tell."

Sarah politely declined his offer and got up to clear the dishes. She was determined to keep to herself any secrets he hadn't discovered the night before, which she was sure didn't leave her with too much to hide. One half-broken heart would probably be able to hold it all.

"Let me do that," he said, rising and taking the plates from her. "You look tired, and I have a feeling I'm going to have a hard time getting to sleep tonight."

If it's any consolation, she thought, *I feel the same way.* But she didn't tell him.

Eight

Sarah was wrong: She slept like a log. She did wake up wrapped around his pillow, but she wasn't going to give the fact any more importance than she had to. Since nobody else had noticed, she figured she was safe. She did entertain thoughts of Colt coming in to wake her, but she sensibly delegated those thoughts to the fantasy file.

Moaning sleepily, she rolled over and checked her clock, then groaned. She didn't have time to waste if she was going to get Atlas open anywhere near nine o'clock.

She found his razor in her bathroom, coffee in the kitchen, and a note stuck to her refrigerator— *I'll bring lunch. Colt*—but the man himself was nowhere in sight. She'd meant what she'd told him, but she hadn't meant to scare him off, even if that might be the smartest move.

His uniform was hanging in her front closet, and his jeans and shirt were neatly folded on the couch, proving he'd definitely moved in. She wondered if she would have been so generous with her home if it hadn't been for the brandy. His jeep was parked outside her gate, and he'd left his black shoes and fancy cowboy boots side by side at her front door. She didn't really think he was running around outside naked and barefoot, but she knew he only had the two changes of clothes. He hadn't expected to stay more than a day and a night.

The mystery remained until she got to the drugstore and the phone started ringing. Tom Jenkins needed a refill on his niacin and added that he'd seen a man just after sunrise that morning, running down the Kent Divide road. He'd looked just like Amanda's boy.

Tom didn't mention anything about the man being naked and barefoot, which was a great relief to Sarah. Then the phone rang again. Phil Dawson had seen him, too, come up on him kind of quick like on that big turn where the Divide road skirted away from the river, and he was just calling to tell Sarah to tell Colt he was damn sorry. He'd have done so himself, but Colt had waved him on and Phil had gotten the idea he hadn't wanted to stop his running. She knew about jogging and all that, Phil was sure, people taking their pulse and whatnot.

Sarah was halfway through her weekly order when the phone rang again. Martha Tully didn't mean to pry, but she'd been a good friend of Amanda's and she'd just seen Colton Haines running by her place when she'd gone down to the road to check the mail. Two of her kids were sick—remember? She'd come in Friday morning for that antibiotic and she hadn't had time to get the mail since, and did Sarah think Colton was okay? Being five miles out of town with nothing but a water bottle and a skimpy pair of shorts and a T-shirt?

Sarah assured Martha on all fronts. Colt Haines did a lot of physical training for his job with the Navy. The man could probably run all day with nothing but a water bottle and a pair of shorts, even skimpy ones. And yes, he was staying with her for the week while he took care of his mother's business. Sarah was sure Ruby was going to keep the beauty shop the same way it had always been. Sarah didn't know if Ruby was going to hire another hair stylist, but she agreed it would be nice to have a manicurist in Rock Creek.

She hung up after checking to see if Martha's kids were still running a fever. They weren't.

Sarah smiled as she rested her hip against the pharmacy counter. California boy. Running across Wyoming like it was a beach or something. She allowed her smile to broaden. He hadn't caused this much of a stir the whole twelve years he'd lived in Rock Creek, except with her.

Colt had raided the R C Grocery for lunch fixings. He made sandwiches out of tenderloin and salad out of fresh fruit, and he put a flank steak in the refrigerator to marinate for tomorrow night. He was trying not to think too much about what he was doing living with Sarah for the week. It wasn't a subject he felt could handle analysis, especially since sleeping together had been wiped off the game plan. Not that he was in the habit of using sex as an excuse for anything, but he'd sure been known to use it as a reason.

He wanted to be with her, a simple enough motivation. It was the why behind the wanting that he was avoiding. On the other hand, he didn't really think they could go all week without making love. It was too good between them. But she'd sounded awfully sure, and she had damn good reasons for not wanting to mess around with him too much.

He finished wrapping the last sandwich and packed the whole lunch into one of the grocery sacks. Truth was, he knew what he was doing. He just wasn't ready to admit to it, because he wasn't sure he believed it. He couldn't have given a guaranteed definition of love if his life depended on it.

He thought about taking wine for lunch, then decided otherwise. She'd just call him California boy again, even though he'd told her he'd spent about the same amount of time in Virginia. He knew it wasn't actually the state she was referring to with her teasing. He'd changed from the boy she'd known, and some of the changes were hard to ignore. He'd seen the world, and she hadn't gotten any farther than Laramie and the University of Wyoming.

He dropped a bag of potato chips in next to the sandwiches. He may have seen the world, but he'd never seen anything as compelling as Sarah asleep with her arms wrapped around the pillow he'd used, a smile playing across her mouth. He'd wanted the right to get in bed with her and make love and babies, not have "sex," as she'd put it. He wanted children, wanted to be a little girl's daddy, wanted to help a boy grow into a man.

He knew losing his mom had shaken up that part of him, had him running scared, but it wasn't just her unexpected death. He'd figured out a couple of years ago that he wasn't immortal. After the shock had worn down, he'd started thinking about his future, but hadn't gotten much further than knowing he didn't want the Navy to be his permanent occupation. When he'd come back two days ago, he hadn't expected Wyoming or Rock Creek to pull on him so hard, to look so much like home. He hadn't expected Sarah.

If he could keep himself from killing her father, they might have a chance.

Sarah checked the clock and eyed the candy counter again. If Colt didn't hurry along, he was going to find his lunch date knee-deep in chocolate bar wrappers and dusted with cookie crumbs.

It was crazy what they were trying to do. Truth be known, she didn't really have as much selfless compassion as she'd been showing him. Yes, she felt badly for him, losing his mom and all. And yes, she was foolishly, powerfully drawn to him. If he gave her even half a reason to do so, she'd probably throw herself at his feet. But he'd left her ten years ago without a word, and what they'd done the other night didn't fit into any decent relationship she knew of. They weren't friends anymore, not the way they'd been before they'd been lovers.

Her father had come home that night ten years ago and told her he'd run the boy off for good, but Sarah hadn't believed him. She hadn't believed him until the months had kept going by, one after the other, and she still hadn't heard from Colt. She'd tried to imagine what her father might have said or done to scare him so badly, but the worst of her imaginings were beyond even her father. And the truth, however painful, had been too obvious to ignore. Colt had told her he was leaving, and nothing they'd done that night had changed his mind. If she had an ounce of sense now, she'd send him packing herself. She didn't want to love him the way she feared she could.

The door opened with a jingle of the bell, and she looked up smiling, knowing it was him. She didn't seem to have an ounce of sense after all.

"I heard you saw quite a bit of country this morning." She came out from behind the cash register and walked by him to put the "Closed" sign on the door.

"Just working out the kinks."

"Ten miles' worth?" She hung the sign and twisted the lock. She'd just take things as they came, she thought. She could do that for a day.

"It was a long night," he said.

"Not as long as they were back in December when the snow hit the bottom of my windowsills," she said, giving him a quick glance. He looked more cowboy than Navy lieutenant at the moment, except for the air of readiness he couldn't seem to leave behind with his uniform. He was more muscular than he'd been as a boy, having finally filled out to the full potential promised by his youth. His narrow-cut western shirt was flame-patterned in shades of blue and purple with black, colors that brought out the clarity and rich darkness of his blue eyes. With effort, she looked away. "Let's eat out on the back porch."

An old white refrigerator stood by the back door, whirring noisily. Sarah grabbed two bottles of soda from it, using the bottle opener on the wall to pop off the tops. Colt held the screen door for her.

"This is nice," he said, gesturing at the cozy alcove built onto the back of the drugstore. The alley was off to the left, Loden's Garage to the right, and dead ahead lay the Great Plains of the West, golden strands of grass shimmering in the sunlight, edged in spring-rain green.

"I've always liked eating out here, but the porch needed a windbreak to make it comfortable." She set the sodas down on the small wooden table shoved against the outside wall and pulled out one of the two chairs. "Of course, in this part of Wyoming *life* needs a windbreak."

She laughed a little, but Colt knew she meant it just the way it sounded. Given the truth of the matter, the obvious question came to mind.

"Why aren't you married, Sarah?"

She didn't meet his gaze, but after a moment she answered.

"It just never happened. What about you? Why aren't you married?" She reached for one of the sandwiches he'd taken out of the grocery sack.

"I was, once."

Her fingers never even got close to the sandwich. It was sheer insanity, the sudden flash of fury roiled up by his admission. He'd gotten married. He'd been married. There had been a Mrs. Colton Haines, and it hadn't been her.

So much for just taking things as they came.

"Excuse me," she said, and removed herself from the table, the porch, and his presence.

She let the screen door slap shut behind her and took one step inside the drugstore. There she stopped, her hand reaching for the old refrigerator for support. Her eyes were squeezed shut, her mouth frozen in a thin, tight line.

The bastard. The yellow-bellied, snake-eyed, fornicating philanderer had been married. He'd taken a woman to wife. There seemed to be no end to the ways he could hurt her.

She was being unreasonable. She knew it, and she didn't give a damn. She heard him coming and hurried farther into the store. She couldn't face him like this. She didn't want to see him ever again.

She wasn't given a choice. He grabbed her from behind and swung her around, his hands gentle but insistent.

"Are you okay?"

"I'm fine." With great effort, she managed to get the words to sound right.

"I didn't mean to upset you."

How incredibly thoughtful of him. "You didn't upset me. I just remembered Jean Clymer is coming by to pick up a prescription. I promised her I'd have it ready."

"Are you sure?"

She didn't answer for a minute, feeling lockjaw set in while she fought and lost the battle of acceptable conduct.

"No," she finally said. "No, I'm not at all sure. I'm just an idiot with a five-year degree from the University of Wyoming who runs her own business and was getting along pretty good until *you* showed up." She glared at him, jerking her arm free.

"Sarah." He reached for her again, but she shook him off.

"Go back to your wife." She took a step backward.

"Ex-wife."

"I don't care." She was horrified to hear her voice falter.

"I was young, Sarah. The situation probably wasn't what you're thinking." He kept coming for her, and she kept slipping away, stepping around him until she was back where she'd started.

"Young?" She pinned him with another glare. "How young? You were twenty when you left, when you asked *me* to marry you, but that didn't count, did it? No. I was just some small-town girl you thought you could use—"

"Don't," he commanded, pushing her back against the refrigerator, his voice quietly furious. And it was a command, given in a tone she instinctively knew was unused to disobedience.

Well, he could get used to it.

"—the same way you used me the other night. I'm so glad I could be of *service* to you."

"Dammit, Sarah." His face was close to hers. His hands were tight around her arms, his fingers biting into her flesh.

"You're hurting me." She looked down to where his hands gripped her, large and darkly tanned against the white material of her pharmacy jacket. She was going to cry again, and she hated him for doing that to her. "Let go of me, you . . . you . . . Let go of me."

She struggled against him, landing an ineffectual blow on his chest. It was like hitting the proverbial brick wall, and that made her angrier, angry enough to cry.

"You liar." She came up with the word while she wiped at a tear running down her face.

The soft sound of his laughter jerked her head back up. With one look, though, she saw it was laughter of the most self-deprecating kind, laughter born of soul deep frustration. He rested his forehead on hers, closing his eyes, and his hold on her gentled.

"God, Sarah. I don't know what to do with us." His hands stroked her arms. "Making love makes you feel helpless, and it's the only time I feel like I know what's going on. For me, being like this is helplessness. Never wanting to, but always hurting you. How can that happen? How can I hurt you so much, when all I want is to hold you and keep you close and safe? How can I hurt you, when all I want to do is love you?" He slipped his arms around her and gathered her within his embrace.

She didn't have any answers for him, but she let him hold her, and his warmth and his words took the anger out of her. She sighed, a rough, ragged sound, and rested her head against his chest.

The refrigerator fan whirred along, the only sound other than their breathing. He kissed her temple and lowered his head to the crook of her neck, but he didn't kiss her again. He only held her, soothing her with his hands in long, even strokes.

Minutes passed as she relaxed against him and drew closer to him in her heart, irresistibly moved to be a part of him. He wanted to love her and maybe didn't. She didn't want to love him and probably had never stopped. She sighed again and turned her face the other way, toward him.

His stomach rumbled, and she hid her face in his shirt.

"Don't worry. I'm not going to faint or anything," he assured her.

"Maybe you should tell me about her."

"My ex-wife?"

She nodded.

"It's not a long story, but if you'll let me eat while I do it, I'll try to drag it out as much as possible."

"You've got a deal," she said, hoping she was up to hearing even a short story of how he'd loved someone else enough to marry her.

He pushed open the screen door and led her out, stopping once to steal a kiss from her mouth. It was a full-scale invasion, hot and sweet, but short, like a surprise attack, and sexual in the way only he could make her feel. Their eyes met for a moment, hers startled and his teasing, and he kissed her on the cheek, a gesture of chaste affection. Without hardly trying, he had her going in a thousand different directions. Like him, she admitted, she didn't know what to do with the two of them.

"Her name was Sumi," he said after they were settled at the table.

"Sumi?" Sarah repeated, forcing herself to glance up at him from her sandwich, as if the information was only mildly interesting and not in any way hurtful. "That's an unusual name."

"No, not unusual, Japanese."

Sarah's glance held as visions of a delicate, dark-eyed woman, coy and graceful, danced across her mind. She heard soft laughter and the rustle of silk, and saw lustrous lengths of jet-black hair cascading over slender olive-skinned shoulders. No wonder he'd been gone for ten years. Damn him.

She looked away, wishing she hadn't asked. She didn't know what she'd expected, but a mysterious, exotic wife was harder on her confidence than the suspected California girl would probably have been.

"It's a very pretty name," she said, going about the business of organizing her sandwich and fruit salad, transferring a few potato chips to her napkin, and generally ignoring him.

"She was pregnant."

The potato chips disintegrated in her fist, and he was rude enough to notice. He picked up her hand and brushed off the crumbs.

"By another sailor, a friend of mine," he went on dryly. "She was desperate. Her family had ostracized her, virtually put her out on the street."

"Why didn't your friend marry her?"

"He was already married, had a wife and two kids in Bremerton."

"I still don't understand why you married her," she said, slapping a few more chips onto her napkin. And she didn't. She didn't understand it at all.

"Believe me. If I had it to do over again, I'd walk away and never look back."

"That bad?" she asked with a lift of her eyebrows, hoping against hope.

"Not exactly. It's just that it got a little more complicated than I had expected. And the Navy sure as hell didn't like it."

He was blushing. She was sure of it. The faintest touch of color edged his cheekbones.

"I don't want you to think I'm some kind of a saint," he added.

Actually, he was in little danger of her thinking he was a saint, and she was just about to tell him, when he continued.

"Of course, after the baby was born, we didn't get within ten feet of each other. She didn't want any more accidents, especially since we'd agreed the marriage would only last a short while after the birth. She didn't want any doubts about the baby's legitimacy, but she didn't want to be married to an American any longer than necessary either."

"She must have been very pretty." A ridiculous statement, but it was the best she could come up with, considering how very glad she was that they'd had enough sense to stop sleeping together after the baby had been born, and how very glad she was that he hadn't withheld this vital bit of information.

"I remember thinking so at the time," he said, sending her a quick, unreadable glance. "We certainly weren't in love, but we got along well enough until she could get her life organized."

"What happened to her?" She had to know, no matter what else she felt, which was mostly aching disappointment. She was supposed to have been the one and only Mrs. Colton Haines.

"You have to understand that she had an unconventional streak in her, or she wouldn't have gotten mixed up with an American sailor in the first place. She came from a good family. Sumi was the outstanding scandal in generations of Sunakawas."

"What happened to her?" Sarah repeated, irritated by his apparent protectiveness.

He hesitated a moment longer before finally answering.

"In essence, she sold herself to the highest bidder."

Sarah mulled his explanation over for a minute, trying and failing to keep a stunned expression off her face. What he'd said sounded too horrible to contemplate.

"You let her do this?" She couldn't help sounding condemning.

"Let her?" he said, looking surprised. "I couldn't have stopped her. She knew she was ruined for a traditional Japanese marriage. She took what she considered the next best thing, which wasn't marriage to a Yankee sailor. She was right. Everything has turned out very well for her."

"How?" Sarah asked, her eyes widening in disbelief. She couldn't imagine how anything as awful as selling yourself could work out well in any context.

"She became the mistress of a high-up executive in one of the car-manufacturing companies. Stood by him when he hit bottom on charges of corporate espionage in his division, and was there to ride the crest of the wave when he came back on top. The ordeal killed him, but not before he'd settled her in Hawaii with a house and a few good investments worth about a half a million dollars."

"And the child?" Sarah asked, not quite hiding the skepticism she was beginning to feel.

"Lives with Sumi and Sumi's mother in Hawaii, on Oahu. Sumi sells real estate."

"Colton Haines, I have never heard so much out-and-out bull in my whole life." *He must think she was a total fool.* "If you don't want to tell me about your wife, don't. I don't care. I don't even think you were married, if that's the best you can come up with. Why, I never—"

"Sumi Sunakawa Haines," he interrupted. "If you ever get to Oahu, you can look her up, or give her a call. She'd know you right off. I told her all about you."

"Oh, I'm sure you did." She let out an exasperated sigh and shoved a bite of sandwich into her mouth.

"It's early in Hawaii. We could call her now."

"I most certainly will not," she mumbled around her sandwich.

"Just don't go on about the doings in Rock Creek. She got so tired of hearing about this place. 'Lock Leek! Lock Leek, Wo-ming! All you ever talk, Cote, is Lock Leek!'" He mimicked a high female voice, ending with a laugh. Then, resting his chin in his hand, he gave Sarah a long, thoughtful look. "She never got tired of hearing about you, though."

"I bet," Sarah said, stabbing a slice of banana out of her fruit salad, still not believing him.

"A man called this morning," he said unexpectedly, "while I was making the coffee. He left a message on your machine. Somebody named Hank."

He was watching her. She could feel his gaze warming her skin into an embarrassed blush.

"He said he was going to ride at Gillette Friday and Saturday, and wondered if you'd like to come up and give him some luck. He promised to be good, and he called you 'honey' a lot."

That was Hank, all right. He always called her honey, and he always promised to be good. But he was too wild even to know what being good meant.

"I should have figured," Colt went on, "there'd be a rodeo cowboy in your life somewhere along the line."

"Hank isn't exactly 'in my life.' He just gets lonely sometimes, but not often enough to do anything permanent about it."

"Is he the reason you're not married?"

She could have laughed at the irony of Colton Haines asking such a crazy question of her, but she didn't.

"No," she said, shaking her head. "I knew right off that Hank was missing whatever parts make a person want to settle down." She waited a moment, then slanted a glance up at him. "A half a million dollars in real estate and investments?"

He nodded.

"She must have been *very* pretty," she said, not feeling the least bit ridiculous this time.

He laughed and reached for her, caressing her cheek with his thumb. "I remember thinking so at the time."

Nine

Ten o'clock was bedtime, had been for years, ever since Sarah was sixteen. She didn't always last until ten, but she seldom lasted longer, unless she was out on a date or at a party. It was a rare evening at home when the news signed off before she did. The nights when there had been a man in her house after ten o'clock were even rarer.

She finished drying a coffee cup and shoved it in the cupboard, not because she was excessively tidy and couldn't go to bed until every last dish was washed, but because having Colton Haines wandering around her house made even thinking about going to bed an emotional mine field.

They'd reached an understanding of sorts over lunch, though she'd be hard-pressed to explain it to anyone, including herself. He'd done a few odd jobs around the drugstore to pass away the afternoon, heavy jobs she'd been putting off for months. After closing time, he'd helped her with her deliveries and taken her to supper at the cafe.

He'd touched her a lot and kissed her more than once, more than twice. Natural, easy, undemanding kisses that had started a fire in her regardless of their simplicity.

She was restless, and it was his fault. He was the cause and the cure, and she wasn't going into the living room to say good night until she was damn sure she could do it without looking wistful.

She grabbed another cup out of the dish drainer and roughed it up with the towel. Despite their nebulous understanding, he'd still made no promises, no suggestions or references to anything beyond the moment, and her survival instincts had responded by pumping up to fighting strength. If she didn't have his love or commitment, she would at least have his respect.

An unusual grating noise intruded on her thoughts. She stopped in mid-swipe and turned her head toward the rest of the house. The sound came again—from the living room, she was sure. Colt had been rewiring her floor lamp earlier, but she didn't think he needed to saw it in half. She wasn't sure she even had a hacksaw in the toolbox he'd dragged out of the garage.

Carrying the cup and the towel, she wandered over to the doorway leading to the living room. One look took all the fight out of her. She leaned her head against the door frame and let the towel trail down her side. He was sprawled across the coach, his head back on the arm, snoring away.

Sighing, she turned back to the kitchen and set the cup and the towel on the table. It was obviously safe to go to bed. She could look at him as wistfully as she wanted and not worry about handling his response.

Sometime later, she woke to the sound of the shower running. A quick glance over her shoulder proved the bathroom light was on. She checked her clock. Not quite midnight.

She must have drifted off, because the next thing she knew she was waking again, rolling over to answer something he'd asked.

"Colt?"

He was silhouetted in her bedroom doorway, one hand dragging through his hair, wearing nothing but his laundered running shorts.

"I had a hell of a night last night," he said, "out there on the couch. I'd really like to sleep in here tonight, if that's okay with you."

"Sure," she mumbled after taking a few moments to assimilate his request. "I don't mind the couch." At least she didn't think she did. She'd never slept on her couch. She had another bedroom in the house, but lacking another bed, she used the space for storage. Her visitors had always made do with the couch, and thus far he was the only one who'd complained.

"No," he said, coming inside the room. "That's not what I meant. I want to sleep with you. I don't really much care where we do it."

His voice was husky with an emotion she couldn't read, but she got the feeling the admission he was making came from a need far deeper than desire. She wasn't sure what to say.

"Don't worry," he went on. "I won't do what I did the other night. I know I was unfair. I know I pushed you, no matter what you said later. Tonight I just want to hold you, to feel you next to me in the night."

She lay in the darkness, letting the silence

stretch and build between them, wishing she could say no, wishing she didn't want to hold him too. When she heard him take the final steps to the bed, she didn't protest. Instead, she rolled over and welcomed him, drawing him close to the place she'd made warm.

He slipped in next to her, pulling the covers back over them. His hand rested naturally on her waist. Their legs slid naturally across each other, fitting together. She felt the beginnings of his arousal when he nestled against her, but he quieted her with a kiss and told her not to worry.

She wasn't worried.

She brushed her mouth across his cheek and caressed his arm. She touched him and kissed him again, and she put his hand on her breast.

"Colt, please," she whispered. She wanted to love him and never have him leave. She wanted to get as close to him as possible. She wanted to remember everything they'd ever been to each other and forget everything they weren't.

He was the only true love she'd ever known. He was the man she'd held in her heart, the only man she'd ever cried over. Loving him had been a burden for ten years, but he was also strength and passion to her. He was an infusion of heat in a life yearning to push the cold emptiness aside.

He was going to leave her again. She knew that one simple truth like she knew the sun was going to come up in the morning. But maybe . . . "Colt, please," she murmured again, sliding her hand down his belly. Maybe this time he'd leave someone behind for her to love.

• • •

Colt woke with a muffled groan. Sunlight flooded the room, telling him dawn had come and gone without him. He dropped a hand over his eyes. He felt like a truck had rolled over him in the night, but it hadn't been a truck. It had been Sarah, a hundred and some pounds of unleashed sensuality and eroticism. There was a lesson to be learned there, something about asking to share the beds of nice Wyoming girls and having the stamina to survive the consequences.

A grin eased across his face. He wouldn't be running ten miles that morning. He didn't need to; he didn't have a kink left in his body.

She was going to be late getting the drugstore opened. He lifted his arm and checked the time on his watch. It was only a quarter to eight, and the drugstore was only five minutes away, but he had a feeling she was going to be late.

Her head was tucked under his chin, her breath warm against his chest. Without hardly moving, he wove the fingers of his other hand through the long, silky hair cascading down her back. Some of the golden strands slipped off her shoulder and onto his abdomen. One of her legs was slung across both of his, her thigh strategically placed to caress him with a single move. After last night, he wouldn't put anything past her, not the deliberate placement and certainly not the move. She'd made moves on him last night that had put a new edge on the word "thrill."

Just thinking about it made any action on her part unnecessary. With the utmost care, he shifted his weight and rolled her beneath him. He didn't want her to wake, not yet, not until he was inside her.

He gently stroked between her thighs, a feather touch meant only to invade her dreams and remind her of him. With each succeeding caress, he increased the contact, explored farther and dared more, until he caught the hint of a smile on her lips and felt her woman's nectar on his fingers. Then he slipped inside, burying himself to the hilt, and waited.

He waited until he saw the color rise in her skin, flushing her to a rosy hue. He waited until her breasts rose and fell with deeper breaths, until her lips parted on a moaning sigh and her eyes fluttered open, gray and luminous, and drenched with the sensations pulsing through her from him.

Sunlight caught in the pale strands of her hair and cast golden shadows in the curve of her neck. Her shoulders were slender and lightly dusted with freckles. Her breasts were tipped in the sweetest pink and beautifully rounded. How could he tell her how much he loved her? He didn't know where to begin.

She opened her mouth to speak, but he silenced her with a shake of his head. She started to move against him, but he stilled her with a hand on her hip.

He held her slumberous gaze with his as the seconds passed, watching her, suffering with her the pleasure of being filled without being taken. She was heavenly to hold, more so than the angel of mercy she'd been the first night, more so than any other woman had ever been. Her softness seduced him on the most basic levels. His need to protect her flowed through him with every breath, yet he knew he was the most dangerous thing in her life. She didn't need his speed with a weapon or his fighting skills, but he needed something from her. He needed the intrinsic connection between them, the healing power of her love, the melding of male and female. No one gave it to him better. No one drew him deeper into the miracle.

She moved against him, and he responded with a slow, deep thrust. His name whispered from her lips. He hushed her with a soft kiss and stroked his tongue along her mouth. He held her until she trembled, until the excitement building in his loins couldn't be held back. Then he covered her mouth with his and took her with him to the secret place they shared.

Mid-morning sunlight slanted through the trees, casting long shadows across the road as Colt and Sarah walked toward town, hand in hand. She was already late opening the drugstore, so she didn't bother to hurry him along. She enjoyed holding his hand too much.

"Daniel called while you were in the shower," he said, guiding her around a muddy patch in the road. "I thought I'd go out to the ranch tomorrow, help him with branding."

"That ought to be fun," she said, mocking him with a roll of her eyes.

He laughed. "You always were kind of squeamish for a country girl."

"Squeamish? Just because I don't like the smell of burning cowhide and the sound of all those calves bawling their little hearts out?"

He chuckled and leaned over to kiss the top of

her head. They walked along in silence for a while before he spoke again.

"I met his wife, Ellen, at the church. She seems real nice."

"She is. She's the one who didn't get me drunk the other night."

"Yeah. I figured that out. Daniel said you two were good friends. He asked if we would like to come to supper this weekend."

It was a perfectly reasonable invitation, delivered matter-of-factly, but her heart stopped for a second. It was one thing for her and Colt to live in a private fantasy world of no tomorrows, and quite another to let other people in, to become a social "we."

"What did you tell him?" she asked when she was sure her voice could match his casual tone. She wasn't about to get her hopes blown all out of proportion by a supper invitation.

"I told him it sounded great, but I'd check with you and get back to him, in case you already had plans for the weekend." He paused for a moment, his hand tightening around hers. "Then I got to thinking that since you invited me to stay until Sunday, you probably hadn't made any other plans. Or if you had, like going to Gillette or something, that maybe I could talk you out of them and we could go have dinner with Daniel and Ellen. I think it would be fun."

"So do I," she said, looking up at him and letting her guard slip another notch.

"Thanks," he said with a quick grin.

They walked on past the corner, silently agreeing to stick to the outskirts of town until they got to the cross street bordering Atlas Drugs. With each step they took, Sarah felt a change take place in him. He held her hand more gently, caressing it with his thumb, and his manner grew hesitant. Finally he stopped on the edge of the road and turned her toward him. His smile was gone, and his eyes were intent and strangely vulnerable.

"I don't know how many promises I can make to you, Sarah. I don't know how many I can keep."

"I haven't asked for any promises," she said, her voice soft with surprise. Then reality took a firm hold. "But you can't blame me for wanting. You can't blame me for that."

A wry smile curved his mouth, and he shook his head. "I wouldn't blame you if you killed me in my sleep. Believe me, Sarah, I know what you're giving up to have me around. I haven't forgotten everything I ever knew about you, about the kind of woman you are."

"What kind of woman is that?"

"The kind who deserves every promise a man can make." He pulled her closer as he spoke, until his mouth was even with her ear and his arms were wrapped around her. "The kind of woman who deserves not to have those promises broken."

He held her for a long time, and she let herself feel secure in his arms, forgetting her own promise not to fall in love, not to let him break her heart.

After they opened the drugstore, he went over to see Ruby. He hadn't wanted to—Sarah had felt his reluctance the moment he'd mentioned going over to the beauty shop—but he had an obligation and he'd gone.

She watched him cross the street, spring sunshine turning his hair pale gold, his stride graceful and determined. She knew Ruby, and she knew there would be tears. She only hoped there wouldn't be any recriminations for his long absence from Rock Creek.

Colt hadn't abandoned his mother. He'd paid for Amanda to visit him in Europe and at his stateside bases. Sarah knew his mom had seen him every year after the first few years of near-absolute silence. But he'd never come home, and she was starting not to care so much what his reasons had been for leaving the way he had.

He returned to the store in time for lunch, looking worse for wear, by her estimation.

"How's Ruby?" she asked.

"Not so good," he said, sliding onto one of the bar stools fronting the Atlas soda fountain. She'd stopped serving sodas and shakes a long time ago. There wasn't enough call for them, and her customers got by with prepackaged ice cream treats out of the old refrigerator's freezer. "She wants me to go out to Mom's trailer with her and sort through some stuff, tell her what to do with things."

He didn't look at all pleased with the idea, and his next statement confirmed her suspicion.

"I told her she could do whatever she wanted with the stuff, but she can't, or won't, accept that as an answer."

"She's right, Colt." Sarah didn't know if it was her place to tell him the facts of life and death, but somebody had to explain a few things to the man. "I'm sure there are things out there you'll want to keep. Things that belonged to your mother, like some of the furniture. And the clothes should be gone through."

"I'm not going through my mom's clothes," he told her with finality.

"The church will be glad to take them, but there might be something special, something—"

"Sarah," he interrupted, flashing her an angry glance.

"Okay, Colt," she said after a short pause, her confusion evident from her tone.

"Look, it's not—" He stopped and swore as he turned away. He swore again and briefly covered his eyes with a hand before he looked back up. "Look, it's not what you think. I know about death, and I know she's gone, but I don't think that means I have to go out there and package up her life and put it all away. I own the land and she left me the trailer. Nobody is going to go out there and take the place. Nobody is going to need her closets."

Sarah heard every word he said and most of the ones he didn't say, and calmly took them all one step further. "I'll go out with Ruby."

"Thank you."

"The Middle East is a mess, easily the most dangerous place I've been, with South America running a close second. Except for this little place in the desert north of Tucson." Colt popped the tops off two bottles of beer and handed Sarah one. They were sitting on her back porch, a screened-in area off the laundry room and kitchen, waiting for the coals in the grill to burn down. The porch door had fallen off its hinges years ago and lay propped against the outside wall. Paint peeled on the empty jamb.

"Tucson, Arizona?" she asked. "What's dangerous about Tucson?"

The sun was getting ready to set, hanging over the prairie with a tenacious, golden grip before dropping off behind the mountains. Colt angled his chair back and stretched one leg across the edge of the iron patio table as he finished up a long swallow of beer.

"We were crawling across the desert in the middle of the night, no moon," he began, tilting his head in her direction. "It was pretty slow going, but we were getting close to our objective, when we came up out of this arroyo and I grabbed on to a pile of coils with fangs on one end and a rattle on the other." He grinned at her shudder of revulsion. "Scared the hell out of me, I guarantee."

"What did you do?"

"Well, I was pretty young, pretty fresh, and I blew its head off before I even thought about what I was doing. Almost shot myself in the hand." He laughed and took another swallow of beer. "If you ever hear any of the guys call me Rattler, you'll know what they're talking about. The new men always think it's a cool name, a good handle, but it's really about me and the snake that almost ate my lunch."

He laughed again, and Sarah smiled. Despite what he said, she guessed he thought it was a cool name too. He wasn't so different from the boy he'd been. The arrogance was still there, heightened by the confidence and success of becoming one of the best. But it wasn't unbearable, and he still had that rare strain of sweetness running through him that had made her fall in love with him the first time.

She only hoped she got the chance to hear one of his friends call him Rattler. As of yet, he hadn't given her any reason to think she might, and she wouldn't be the one to broach the subject. She was determined to hold on to that one bit of pride—and to whatever else the good Lord sent her way.

Her hand absently slid across her tummy. He'd talked about being unfair, but he was no match for her. Her time was right, her body's cycle turning with the tides and her own fervent wish. The rest was up to Mother Nature.

When the coals were an ashy gray, Colt went inside to get the flank steak he'd been marinating for the last two days. Sarah relaxed back in her chair, but barely got comfortable before imminent disaster caught her eye. She jumped up with a silent curse on her lips as a red-and-white truck pulled off the street and cut across the empty lot between her house and the Davis place. The pickup bounced through the weeds and ruts, tearing up a dust cloud and adding another layer of dirt to the vehicle. There was no mistaking the driver—Hank Cavanaugh, professional rodeo cowboy, saddle-bronc and bareback rider extraordinaire.

He pulled to a stop at her back fence, and the cloud of dust blew on past the truck, heading toward Nebraska. With a natural, easy athletic ability, he stepped from the open pickup door to the top of her fence, and on down the other side into her yard. He was the only man she knew who could juggle and ride a unicycle at the same time.

He was also the only man she knew who had tried, or who wanted to do it enough to spend hours practicing the double trick. He swore it made him a better bronc rider, and he was probably right. The only time she'd ever seen him serious about anything was the time she'd been behind the bucking chutes, before he rode a bronc, and watched him work his hand into his rigging. For a moment, she'd seen another side of him, and she'd almost fallen in love. But eight seconds later, he'd been the same wild Hank, looking for a good time and willing to share it with anyone who came down the pike.

"Howdy, Miss Sarah," he called, a teasing twinkle lighting his dark eyes, his voice a sexy drawl meant to warn her of his mood.

Sarah was tempted to run, actually run, but she knew Hank. If she ran, he'd chase. Mostly he had it the other way, with the women chasing after him. They couldn't resist his crooked smile and good looks, and his natural shyness with most females.

"Hey, Hank. I got your message." She took a step back on the porch; she couldn't help herself. "I didn't expect you to be coming through till—"

Her next words were swallowed up by her squeal of protest as he bounded up the steps and swung her over his shoulder. He was five feet eight inches and a hundred and fifty pounds of lean hardness, near perfect for riding broncs or bulls, though he'd given up the bulls a few years back.

He laughed and turned his head to gently bite her hip through her jeans. "Miss Sarah, I do declare, you get sweeter every time I haul through here."

"Put me down, Hank." She squirmed in his grip.

"Have you been following me in the *Prorodeo Sports News*? This is the year I make the National Finals. You gonna come to Vegas if I do?"

"If you put me down, I might consider it." She stopped squirming and waited.

"Well, I don't know, honey. This is about as close as you ever let . . ."

The sudden quieting of his voice was ominous and made Sarah's heart speed up. She couldn't see a thing except for his cute backside and the heels of his boots, slung over his shoulder the way she was. But she could imagine plenty, and his next words lent a lot of credence to her imagination.

"Hi, I'm Hank Cavanaugh." She felt his weight shift beneath her as he took a step forward and stretched out a friendly hand. His other arm tightened around her thighs so as not to lose her.

"Colton Haines," Colt answered, making her humiliation complete.

"Hank, put me down."

"Oh, sure, honey," he said, as if suddenly remembering he was carrying her around. When her feet touched the porch floor, he turned his attention back to Colt, but kept his arm around her waist. "I know a Haines from Belle Fourche in South Dakota—a team roper. I used to run into him a lot on the Badlands Circuit."

Sarah extricated herself from his hold, asking if he'd like a beer.

"Sure, honey. That would be great." Hank grinned and gave her a gentle swat. He was pushing his luck, and judging by his grin he knew it. But pushing luck was his business.

By the time she got back, they had apparently decided Colt wasn't related to the roping Belle Fourche Haineses, and had moved on to a subject near and dear to Hank's heart—the piece of junk he had stockpiled next to her garage the previous Thanksgiving.

"Last time I was here," Hank was telling Colt, "I bought a wrecked horse trailer from Al Loden over at the garage. Got most of it tore down, the good parts anyway. There's a man up in Gillette who'll buy it off me, if I could get it loaded into the bed of my pickup."

"Sure," Colt answered. "I'd be glad to help."

Hank grinned and winked at her. "This is great. It's out back of Sarah's garage. I'll just pull my truck around."

The cowboy could charm snakes, even a rattler.

Ten

Sarah was supposed to watch the steak while the two men stacked big pieces of metal into the bed of Hank's pickup, but mostly she watched them. They seemed to be getting along real well. It was disconcerting.

The steak was done long before they were, and when she saw the two of them laughing—Hank so hard he almost dropped his half of one of the trailer panels—she gave up and took herself and the slab of charred meat inside. Colt had known her for years and been living with her for three days, and she hadn't been able to make him laugh. She knew the circumstances were difficult, but it still bothered her that he was laughing with Hank.

"I swear to God, Colton," Hank said. "You can check it out yourself, next time you get to Abilene." He nodded to Colt, and together they heaved the panel into the truck. Metal hit metal with a clatter and a clang.

Colt moved back from the truck, still grinning. "I'll have to take your word for it. I don't think I'll be getting to Abilene."

"Well, you've got the look of somebody who's going somewhere." Hank leaned over the truck bed and pushed his worn white cowboy hat to the back of his head. "I don't suppose you'll be taking Sarah with you."

"Why wouldn't you suppose that?" Colt asked, disturbed by the younger man's perceptiveness and sudden change in subject.

Hank glanced back at the house, then turned and met Colt's gaze. "She looked kinda sad to me. I figure that has something to do with you, seeing as how this is the first time I've ever shown up and found another man hanging around."

Colt didn't have a reply. Hank had hit too close to the truth. He knew he was being selfish, taking her love and her loving without making some sort of commitment, saying something about tomorrow or the week after next. But he didn't think getting down on his knees and begging her to come to California with him was the right thing to do. They weren't kids anymore—she'd been right about that—and the United States Navy didn't give him much room to compromise.

He knew he'd return to her. But their emotions were running hot, too hot to think straight and make decisions right now.

"Don't get me wrong," Hank said into the silence. "I don't mind you leaving. I don't mind it at all." A broad grin flashed across his deeply tanned face. "Matter of fact, if I thought I could do it, I'd run you off myself. I'm not planning on being a good-for-nothing rodeo cowboy my whole life. One of these days I'll be a good-for-something rodeo cowboy, and Sarah is just about the best thing I've found since I've been going down the road."

Colt had a feeling he knew where the conversation was heading. He couldn't say he liked it, but neither did he stop it.

Hank shrugged and looked out over the prairie. "In kind of a strange way, I've always been glad she was too smart to give in to me. I've always been a little on the untamed side, and I figured if she had enough sense not to sleep with me, she probably wasn't sleeping with any of the other ramrods who blow through Rock Creek." He paused and gave Colt a shrewd glance from beneath the brim of his hat. "But she's sleeping with you . . . and you're breaking her heart."

Colt had been right: The kid had played him like a raw recruit, and he hadn't missed a trick. "Are you sure you don't want to run me out of town?"

Hank laughed and shook his head. "No. I've already paid for a couple of broncs to try to bust me up in Gillette. I don't think I'll give you the same chance for free. 'Cause something tells me that the chances I take for fun, you take for a living, and taking chances for a living makes people so damned serious, and maybe a bit dangerous."

"How did you figure that out?" If the cowboy was half as good at reading his horses as he'd been at reading Sarah and him, Colt thought, then he probably *would* get to the National Finals.

"That's an Air Force jeep over there," Hank said, "and you don't look like a desk jockey. You're too ready, like you're used to things happening fast. You'd probably make a good bronc rider."

"And you'd make a good psychiatrist, or an intelligence operative." Colt let out a short laugh despite himself, and gave the younger man a closer look. "Maybe I ought to be the one running you out of town."

"If I didn't think that no matter how much damage we might do to each other, it would be Sarah who was hurt the most, I might give you a try." Hank smiled, slow and easy, and adjusted his hat back down on his forehead.

Colt laughed again and wished he didn't like Hank Cavanaugh nearly as much as he did. "Just to set the record straight, I'm Navy, not Air Force."

"That's still an Air Force jeep." Hank leaned back and looked over at the vehicle parked in the driveway.

"Yeah. It is."

"Then you must be real good at something," Hank said, with just enough doubt to gall Colt into answering.

"I get in, get the job done, and get out alive, and I've done it enough times that every now and then somebody does me a favor."

"I suppose I ought to be grateful we're not going to wrestle it out right here in this patch of weeds." Hank's voice was thoughtful, but still damnably unconvinced.

Colt decided to convince him, to save both of them any trouble. Young men were always more ready to fight than made sense, which, of course, was one of the basic tenets of the military.

"Well, Hank, I'll tell you. I'm basically the property of the United States government, and I have an obligation to the taxpayers. If I thought you were going to get serious, we'd never get to the wrestling part. The Navy has spent an awful lot of time and money teaching me how to stay out of trouble. Sometimes that's not so good for the other guy." He stopped to let his words sink in, then continued. "On the other hand, we could do this the fair way. You go back to San Diego with me, join the Navy, try for the teams, and spend six months working out in the Silver Strand, then we come back to this patch of weeds and see who comes out on top. My guess is it would be even money at that point." And that was the only point he was going to concede to the wild young cowboy with the bright, easy smile and the hots for Sarah. "Are you staying for supper?"

"No," Hank said slowly. "I don't think so. I think I'll go ahead on up to Gillette. But I want you to know, Colton, after you're gone, I'll be back."

Hank's parting words all but ruined Colt's appetite. He stabbed a piece of steak and sat there staring at it. He'd come back to Rock Creek wanting to be with her, needing to be with her. He hadn't thought of anyone else wanting and needing the same thing. In truth, he hadn't even thought about what Sarah might be wanting or needing. She'd taken him in, and he'd been satisfied.

He hadn't minded Hank's phone message. He hadn't considered a western drawl on a tape machine competition, not when he was the man who was with her. But the difference between a recorded voice and a man showing up looking cocky and being intelligent was undeniable.

Cole wanted Sarah, wanted to bask in the forgiveness and generosity of her love. He hadn't wanted to face realities and make plans. His life was full of harsh realities. He'd wanted a reprieve. Losing his mom was taking a deep, silent toll, and he needed time. He didn't want to have to think about losing Sarah too.

He'd caught a glimpse of her father when he'd gone over to see Ruby. Bull had been leaving the cafe, walking with a couple of other men to a line of pickup trucks parked on the street.

He wasn't through with Bull Brooks, and that was the biggest reason he should get out of town without commitments. Sarah didn't like her father, but Colt wanted to hurt him.

Controlling his emotions, or at least channeling them for maximum effectiveness, was one of the things that made him good. He'd never equated rashness with courage. He'd never killed a man without his own life being the price of failure. But he'd seen Bulls Brooks crossing a sidewalk in Rock Creek, Wyoming, and he'd gotten a killing urge.

The time his mom had visited him in Virginia, she'd been bruised on one side of her face. Not much, but too darkly to hide with makeup. She'd said she'd taken a fall. He'd called her a liar.

Mothers, it seemed, didn't take kindly to such talk from their sons, no matter how big their boys had gotten over the years. She'd laid down the law and told him his place, which wasn't jumping to conclusions about her private affairs. He'd told her he didn't have to jump too damn far to figure out what was going on, and she'd left town. She'd left him for the bastard who had hit her.

All of Colt's imaginings of ever returning to Rock

Creek had died that day. Yet there he was again, in mind, body, and soul, connected to a Rock Creek woman in ways that defied explanation.

He looked up at her. "Hank said you were engaged when he met you. Wearing a ring the size of Gibraltar." He hadn't wanted to talk about her near marriage, but he wasn't able to ignore it.

Sarah had wondered what was bothering him. She knew she'd burned the flank steak, grilling it long past his instructions of five minutes per side, but his thoughts had seemed to be far beyond the practical consideration of food. And so they had been.

"It was pretty big," she admitted, carefully cutting a piece of meat, putting her full concentration into the action.

"What about the guy?" he asked, the seriousness of his voice giving a ton of weight to the question.

"Jeff?" She cut another piece of meat while she was at it. "Oh, he's not so big. He's built sort of like Hank, but heavier."

His silence told her he didn't think she was funny.

"And he's not nearly as nice," she added, floundering for information to throw into the void. The instant the words were out, though, she knew she couldn't have chosen less wisely. She quickly filled in and covered up with a slew of trivia. "He was a business major at Laramie. I think he went back for his M.B.A., and I heard he's done real well for himself in the rental business. He's got a chain of stores from Rock Springs to Cheyenne, renting all sorts of things, from power rakes to party dishes. We went together mostly while I was still in school, though he graduated a year before me."

"What happened?"

"Between us? Jeff and me?" She glanced at him before busying herself with buttering a roll. "The usual. College romance goes sour, people grow up, go their own ways. Typical situation."

"Did you love him?" Colt knew it sounded like a stupid question, but he didn't withdraw it.

"He wasn't pregnant, if that's what you mean." The look she gave him told him exactly what she thought of his interrogation.

"Hank said he got the impression you weren't too impressed with your fiancé. I just wondered—"

"Hank said that?" she interrupted. When he nodded, she laughed. "Hank was the one who wasn't impressed. I thought Jeff Sanders was a good catch, a man with a future, someone I could count on . . ." Her words slowed as she held his gaze, and he saw indecision flicker in her eyes. She glanced away and finished her sentence. "Until the night he hit me. That changed my mind pretty quick."

He stiffened, bodily and emotionally. "How in the hell did you ever get hooked up with somebody like that?" he demanded, not able to hide his anger or his disbelief.

"He didn't get 'like that' until he put his ring on my finger. Up until then, he'd behaved quite normally."

"And after he hit you the first time?" he asked with difficulty. He didn't understand. He didn't understand any of it.

"After he hit me the first time, the *only* time, I went to this bar in Laramie, looking for somebody with a gun. Instead I found this young cowboy who didn't look old enough to even be in a bar. He had a real sweet smile, no gun, and he wouldn't leave me alone until I told him why my cheek was turning blue and my mouth was cut."

"Hank?"

"Hank. He went with me to Jeff's and stood by me while I gave him back his diamond. Then he followed me to my apartment and slept in his truck for the rest of the night, just to make sure there wasn't any trouble, he said. Later, I found out he'd been sleeping in his truck most of the summer, looking for his first big win. He got it the next night at the Laramie River Rodeo."

"And you've been his good-luck charm ever since," Colt said, doubly grateful he and the bronc rider hadn't gotten uncivilized with each other.

"He likes to tell me so, on the three or four occasions when he comes through town every year."

"He'd come more often if you gave him half a reason," he said, despite himself. Or to spite himself.

A big sigh swelled her chest as she tossed the half-buttered roll down on her plate. "Given your experience, I know this will probably come as a surprise," she said as she pushed away from the table. "But believe it or not, I don't jump into bed with every man who gets a notion." With that, she walked away from her dinner and didn't look back.

He found her a few minutes later, curled up on the porch swing, wrapped in an afghan she'd removed from the couch. She didn't acknowledge his presence by so much as a blink.

"I guess I don't understand how you could get

close to marrying a man like that," he said. It wasn't much as far as apologies or excuses went, but it was the truth.

"I was lonely," she said, her voice tight. "I was twenty years old, going into my junior year of college, and I'd just found out that the boy I'd been waiting two years to hear from had joined the Navy, God knows when, and was shipping out to Japan. The girl who told me, Barb McLaughlin— you remember her from school, I'm sure—she thought it was so exciting. And all I could think was *Japan, Japan,* and die inside."

"Sarah—"

"It was incredibly stupid of me to say yes to Jeff. Talk about love on the rebound. Funny, isn't it. I got engaged hoping for a marriage that would last a lifetime, and you were getting married hoping to get laid for a few months."

"Sarah, stop it."

"Dammit, Colt." She glared up at him, her eyes shining with unshed tears. "If you don't like the answers, quit asking the questions."

She was right. He hadn't made any claims. He didn't deserve more than she wanted to offer, not when she'd given him so much.

"I apologize," he said, "for asking about Jeff. I'm sorry I upset you."

And he was, damn sorry for upsetting her, but his words never seemed to be enough. He stood there, watching her, and knew something else needed to be said, something he'd thought a hundred times in the last few days and over a thousand times ten years ago.

"I'm sorry I left you." His voice grew rough, less sure. "I never wanted to hurt you."

He didn't know what he'd expected those words to get him, but even his lowest hopes weren't met. She rested her cheek on her updrawn knees and looked out on the plains in utter silence.

He needed a beer. No other acceptable thought came to mind. He needed a beer, or six or seven of them, and she needed a shot of Scotch. He went back to the kitchen for both, pouring a double over ice for her and taking his straight from the bottle. If they were going to fight all night, he'd just as soon do it with his senses dulled.

When he sat down on the swing, she scooted farther to her side. He offered her the drink in silence, and she took it in the same manner. The quiet grew around them, leaving plenty of room for the occasional car sound from the main street to make its way over to her house. The Davises called in their dog and turned out their lights. Nothing happened out on the prairie, nothing except the moon and the stars, and the black-velvet darkness of the night.

They both drank, and he pushed the swing. Neither of them said a word. When the temperature became noticeably cooler, she offered him a corner of the afghan, then offered him more. He helped her reorganize the blanket and her position, and she accidentally knocked over his beer bottle.

"Sorry."

"Don't worry about it."

"Can you hold this?"

He took her glass and held up her end of the blanket while she arranged the rest of it over his shoulders. She knelt on the swing to reach around him, leaning over him in all the ways guaranteed *not* to maintain distance and anger and hurt feelings.

"Lift up a little, please."

He did, and she tucked the blanket behind him, between his body and the cold slats of the swing. Her hands touched his shoulders, her breasts brushed his arm, her breath was warm and Scotchy against the side of his face. He held himself in check for as long as he could, until the effort became ludicrous when compared to the comfort he knew would be theirs if he slipped his arms around her and pulled her into his lap.

She slid into place as naturally as water flowing to lower ground, her body relaxing against his with ease and warmth. He held her for a long time, then finished off her drink in one long swallow and set the glass aside. She snuggled closer, and he was content.

When she snuggled again, his contentment began to come apart in the nicest way. He inhaled deeply and stroked his hand down her thigh. Her murmured response encouraged him to do more. Her hand slipping between his legs made the desire a necessity. She couldn't touch him without him needing to touch her.

She teased him, and he unbuttoned her blouse. In moments he was back on solid ground, with Sarah in his arms and the world turning in an ever more benevolent universe.

Eleven

Wednesday nights could be big nights in Rock Creek. On Wednesday nights Guy Hill, owner of the Sagebrush Bar, was sometimes able to entice one of the better Cheyenne bands into town for a few sets and a cut of the take. On weekends Rock Creek had to make do with more local talent, or just less talent, but on a lucky Wednesday it wasn't unheard of for the Sagebrush to have a four- or five-piece group—or at least part of one, because not everyone could be enticed to spend his or her Wednesday hauling across barren country, not even for free beer and cold cash.

Colt and Sarah worked their way through the crowd of folks who had come out midweek to hear The Muleskinners, a band semi-famous throughout most of southern Wyoming and at a few select locations in northern Colorado. A few hellos were exchanged, a few nods, and a couple of offers were made to buy them both a beer.

Colt kept heading her toward the dance floor.

He dropped their coats on an empty table as they passed, and when their feet hit the parquet he turned her into his arms. He'd been out at the Calhoun ranch all day, and he'd missed her.

Sarah was equally glad to get close to him, to feel his arms hold her and his body guide her in an easy, shuffling two-step. One of the beer offers had been from the girls'-night-out contingent, and she knew there hadn't been a woman among them who hadn't been stripping him down to past his skivvies with their eyes. He had the kind of body that did that to women, and the kind of face that made the effort all that much more worthwhile. Not overly handsome or anywhere near pretty, but appealing, with clean lines and uncompromising strength.

She knew they were the talk of the town—some were worried about her sure-to-be-broken heart and some were much less kind. Once or twice she'd wondered what they'd all say if their pharmacist turned up in the family way. Mostly she didn't think about that possibility. Somewhere in her heart, the decision to try had been made before she'd consciously done anything to bring about success. She'd prayed for his child once. It wasn't so hard to ask a second time.

The music changed to a love song about a man telling his sweet darlin' that she'd never get over him, that even if she walked out on him, she'd never get away from him, because she'd be thinking about him all the time, carrying him with her in her thoughts.

Sarah believed every word.

Colt gathered her close and swayed with her to the music, loving the feel of her in his arms, of holding her hand, so small and delicate, in his. He rested his cheek against the top of her head. Her hair was pulled back in a lank ponytail, making a pale stream down the middle of her back. They had four more days together, four more nights. He didn't think it was going to be enough.

He had some leave built up that he should be able to take in a month or two. He could come back, but he wondered how he'd last that long, if the nights would get too lonely, the days too empty.

Maybe it was time for him to start thinking about what Sarah might be wanting. It was impossible for them just to keep going on the way they had been. Reality was bound to intrude, and even if they held it at bay for a while longer, on Sunday it would be standing right on the doorstep as he told Sarah good-bye.

The turn of his thoughts had an unwelcome effect on his perceptions. He slowed the movement of his feet and bent his head deeper into the curve of her neck and shoulder, holding her tighter. Sarah wasn't the one who was hiding from reality. She knew he was leaving. He doubted if she'd forgotten it for a minute, but she'd lowered her guard and let him in to use up her life until he was done, until Sunday.

He had to come back.

The song ended with the band announcing a break. Colt led her back to the table, holding her hand and keeping her close. They'd already decided to stay for only a couple of dances and a beer. He hadn't wanted to come at all, preferring not to make small talk with well-meaning people, preferring the privacy of her company to all others. But Sarah had insisted that they come up for air—her words exactly—and he'd smiled and pulled his boots back on. She'd had a point.

A couple of women he'd noticed sizing him up earlier came over to talk, asking Sarah about some stuff she was special-ordering for them through the drugstore and obviously angling for an introduction. Colt knew their interest in him had more to do with him being a novelty than anything personally intriguing about him. Rock Creek was a small community. Anybody new was bound to stir up interest, especially among the ranks of the unfulfilled. He bowed out of the whole process by asking Sarah what she wanted to drink.

He went up to the bar to get their beers and allowed himself to get roped into a conversation about the feedlot and the best ways to fatten up cattle for market; how if they got a sharp manager in there who bought from the ranchers at the right price and didn't hold the animals too long, and if the prices held at the packing plants, why, anybody should be able to make a profit, right there in Rock Creek. The old-timers were sure of it. America loved beef, and that was that.

"You ran a herd over there on your mom's place, didn't you, Colton?" asked a wizened old geezer with tobacco-stained teeth and squint lines like the canyon lands.

"Yes, sir," Cole replied, digging in his pocket to pay for the beer. "But that's been ten years."

"Cows don't change, son." The old man nodded sagely, and men younger and older on their end of the bar made abstract sounds of agreement. The cows didn't change, and neither did the land, except when people went around putting on improvements for the county to tax.

The conversation took a wide turn through taxes while Colt waited for the bartender to return with his change. But the beef-cattle market was the subject of choice, and pretty soon the group was on it again, going out of their way to include him as a native son.

"Do they feed you Navy boys plenty of beef?"

"Yes, sir. I've had it three meals a day sometimes."

That got a round of approving laughter. The country was in good hands if they were feeding the fighting men beef. They managed to fit in the Japanese taxing beef imports and worked around to Pearl Harbor, which seemed to tie everything together—the beef industry, unreasonable taxes, and for Colt's benefit, the Navy—before the bartender made it back.

Colt dropped a tip on the bar and shoved the rest of the money back in his pocket, figuring he'd been gone long enough for Sarah to have finished her business. He glanced over his shoulder just to check and froze with an instant rush of adrenaline.

He forced himself to breathe, to not react externally, to not overreact to the scene before him. It wasn't against the law for Bull Brooks to talk to his daughter.

Sarah had heard the same speech from her father a hundred times, maybe even a thousand, given her twenty-eight years and his variations on the theme of herself, her mother, and their combined sins. The relentless haranguing was as much a part of her father as his skin or his teeth. He was a natural-born complainer, whose skills had been honed by the injustices of life, most of which—he claimed—had been visited on him by women.

In her relationship with her father, Sarah had gone through the stages of intimidation and anger, then irritation and weariness, and finally boredom and pity. She knew he hated that, and that it got him more riled up with her than was probably healthy for a man with his heart condition. She knew, too, that she should care more than she did. It bothered her sometimes, how little she cared for her own father. Other times, she thought it was probably a healthy attitude: not giving too much credence to a man who abused women.

He had never hit her. He'd saved the physical punishment for her mom. But he'd been yelling at her for as long as she could remember.

He was getting ready to do it again. She could tell by the whine creeping into his voice. Lord, how many times had she asked Guy not to let him get liquored up.

"I told your mother times are tough," he was saying, "and if you would just back me up on this, maybe she'd start to see it clear. It does neither you or me any good to have our money going out of Rock Creek. We're the ones trying to keep the damn place alive."

Truly, this was his most logical argument, Sarah thought. She was tempted to agree with him that he shouldn't have to pay child support, if only so he'd be gone before Colt got back with her drink.

Her father continued, though. "Why a man should have to pay for kids a cheatin' woman steals out from under him makes no damn sense to me. No damn sense a'tall."

His weakest argument to Sarah's way of thinking, considering how long he and Amanda Haines had carried on. She'd often wondered what Amanda had seen in her father, but it was beyond her imagination. Oh, she'd admit he wasn't bad-looking for his age, and he made a better living than most in the county, and she knew some women liked their men rough around the edges. Still, it didn't add up in her book.

Amanda had certainly seemed to have Robert "Bull" Brooks more under her thumb than Sarah's mom had ever managed, and maybe that had been his appeal—the taming of him. She'd never married him either, so maybe he hadn't slapped her around.

"And don't you go trying to pull any fancy tricks on me," Bull said. "I won't put up with it. I won't put up with it for a minute, not one damn minute."

Sarah knew what he was talking about. The previous year she'd devised a grand scheme, whereby she and her mom bypassed Bull in the rent and child support exchange. Sarah paid her mother the money she owed her father for rent on the drugstore, thereby saving her mother the hassle of trying to get child support out of her ex-husband. She'd thought it was a beautiful plan, too perfect to pass up. But Bull had threatened to evict her when he found out.

"The next time you two try any funny business, I'm going into Cheyenne to personally shake the money back out of her. You've got no right to give her my rent."

"Jack will kill you, Bull," Sarah said it as calmly

as Jack, her stepfather, had. "You lay one hand
on her, and he'll kill you."

"That bleeding heart wouldn't kill a chicken to
put meat on his starving family's table. He sure as
hell isn't going to be coming after me with more
than a stack of words."

Jack was a lawyer who did *pro bono* work for
victims of domestic violence. Under most circumstances, she would have agreed with her father.
Jack was the antithesis of a violent man. But Jack
also knew the statistics about who killed women,
and abusive husbands and ex-husbands were at
the top of the list.

"I wouldn't count on it, Bull. I think you'd better
stay out of Cheyenne."

"Dammit, girl!" he exploded in a burst of frus-
trated, drunken fury, his hand banging down on
the table. "Don't you go telling me what—"

One second her father was slamming the table,
and the next he was stretched across it, with Colt
pinning him down.

Colt jerked him back up, but not before Sarah
felt the deadly pall of animosity radiating off the
two men. Her father had gone wild-eyed with fear;
Colt's face was expressionless, yet somehow le-
thal.

"Let's go, old man." Colt jerked her father again,
getting him straighter on his feet, and the two of
them headed for the door just as The Muleskinners broke into a new song.

Sarah wasn't the only person who had seen the
quick action, but the speed of it made it hard to
comprehend. The problem wasn't apparent, and
between the dancers moving to the floor and Colt

and her father moving toward the door, nothing looked terribly amiss—except to Sarah.

She'd never seen her father afraid of anything or anybody in her whole life. He dished out fear; he didn't take delivery. She could imagine what Colt must have seen from his end of the bar and why he'd reacted the way he had, but nothing explained the flash of terror she'd seen in her father's eyes.

Guy had kicked Bull out of the Sagebrush twice that year for getting mean and picking fights. To call him quarrelsome was putting it mildly. But Colt had handed him the perfect excuse for busting into somebody. Yet he'd just laid there on the table, too scared to spit.

She got up from her chair, a half minute behind the two men, trying to pull her thoughts together and get around the people in the bar without bumping into anyone. Somehow Colt had managed not to cause a scene. She didn't want to either, but she had a feeling she'd better get outside quickly.

The night air was cool against her face, especially after the warmth of the crowded bar. She looked north, toward town, and saw nothing but darkness and taillights of a tractor-trailer heading up the highway. South was the Sagebrush parking lot. It took her a moment, but she finally spotted Colt's white shirt, and next to him the smudgier blur of her father's outline. She started forward, following them into the maze of cars and pickup trucks.

Colt recognized Bull's truck from in front of the cafe the other day, and also because of the loops of rawhide silhouetted in the back window. His hand instinctively tightened in the scruff of Bull's shirt. He'd almost talked himself out of doing any physical damage to the older man, but the sight of the whip weighed the scales heavily once more toward mayhem.

Bull hadn't expected him, and Colt had used surprise to get Bull out of the bar in one piece. It wasn't until they'd gotten to the parking lot that the older man had come out of shock and started to struggle.

Even with his age and conditioning advantage, Colt had his hands full. Trying to keep his edge, he gave Bull a shove, sending him flying toward the side of his truck. Bull hit the panel with a thwack, but he only went partway down. When he came up, he had a knife in his hand.

Unlike Bull, Colt didn't allow himself to be surprised. His kick met the tender inside juncture of Bull's wrist and hand before the man got his weapon even waist-high. Colt had started the fight, and he damn well planned on finishing it on top. The knife skittered away into the night, and Colt grabbed Bull and put his face to the pickup door before he could find any more trouble.

"You're on thin ice, *old man*. Don't push me," he warned close to Bull's ear.

"I'll have the law on you, you son of a bitch." Bull hissed the words into the cold metal pressed up against his cheek.

"Whole lot of good that's going to do you if you're dead."

Bull tried to jerk free, but Colt just held him tighter. It wasn't easy. The man was nothing but wiry strength.

"We have unfinished business." Colt pressed him harder into the truck.

"No we don't. I finished with you, boy, and you got no more than you deserved." Bull's voice shook, just as his body was starting to do. Colt took both as signs of weakness and pressed harder.

"I'm not talking about what you did to me. I'm talking about what you tried to do to Sarah." He pulled Bull's arm higher up in the middle of his back, until the man wheezed, and he relished Bull's torment in a way he knew wasn't good. "I'm talking about what you did to your wife, and what you did to my mom, hitting her in the face." His next breath hurt, and suddenly he was surprised, not by Bull, but by himself. "Bruising her, treating her like—" His voice broke. *God.* It took every ounce of concentration he had to keep from snapping Bull's neck. His skin was jumping and his hands ached with the need for action and release.

He closed his eyes against the pain he felt, against new loss and raw emotion, and slowly lowered his brow to the back of Bull's head. His fists tightened in the cloth of the man's shirt. Bull smelled of fear; he was saturated with panic.

Colt's breathing accidentally fell into rhythm with the older man's, and with a silent groan he slammed into Bull's body again, hurting him and knocking him into his own ragged cadence.

He'd shared too much with the man. He'd shared his mother, and he'd shared Sarah, and he'd somehow lost both to Bull Brooks. Now he had his enemy in his hands, straining for escape, and so help him, they were once again sharing pain and fear, just as they had the night Bull had marked him for life.

"You bastard." He couldn't kill him. He couldn't even hurt him in a way that would count, a way that would last. Bull had taken his blood that night. He couldn't return the favor. *"You friggin' bastard."*

He slammed into Bull again, stunning him before he turned and staggered away from the man, away from the whip and past, wishing he could just as easily walk away from the hate.

Sarah had lost them, and saw nothing until she spotted Colt walking away from her father's truck. She heard nothing except what her father cried out at the younger man's back. The violence of the obscenity riveted her to a standstill, and was matched only by the violence of Colt's reaction.

He whirled with a closed hand, backhanding her father and creating a frightening connection of fist and jaw. Bull crumpled to a heap in a slow-motion collapse, his body curving away from the truck to land in the dirt.

Sarah didn't move. Her mind told her to, but her feet didn't get the command. Her gaze went from her father to Colt. He was walking toward her, not looking back to see what damage he had done. He stopped a few feet away.

"You better go check on him. I think I hurt him." His voice was low and steady, and he met her eyes only once before walking on.

She took a step toward her father, then turned quickly to watch Colt a moment longer. A groan forced her attention back to the parking lot.

She knelt by Bull's prone figure, checking him quickly and carefully for major trauma. She found none. He was breathing without too much trouble, and he was pushing himself to all fours, starting to bitch and moan.

"Shut up, Bull," she said. "I don't think he hurt you near as badly as he scared you."

"He broke something in my face. I can feel it." Each of Bull's words came padded on both sides with a thick layer of cursing. It made it damn near impossible for Sarah to understand what he said, but when she did, she gave her own orders.

"Lie back down and stay put." She stood up and checked a couple of pickup beds until she found a horse blanket. She threw it over her father and admonished him one more time to stay put until she could get help. She met Guy Hill halfway back to the bar, and he told her they'd already called Doc Tanner.

The next few hours were awful. Colt had thankfully disappeared—her father didn't have nearly enough fight knocked out of him for Colt to have been anything but a hindrance—and everyone assumed she'd be the one taking care of her father, driving him out to Doc Tanner's and all. Of course, she did it. There didn't seem to be another option, other than letting him rot in the parking lot, which she'd considered more than once while listening to him gripe and swear himself a blue streak.

Doc Tanner tallied up Bull's injuries as two lost teeth and a hairline fracture to the jaw, then sent him home with two prescriptions. Sarah, of course, had to stop at the drugstore to fill them.

By the time she got home, she was a wreck, but the jeep in her driveway and the light in her living room window was all she needed to feel better.

She was going to tease him about being right: They should have stayed home.

Maybe later she would ask him what had happened out in the parking lot. She planned on reassuring him that her father wasn't hurt any worse than he had been after other bar fights. She wanted to check Colt's hand, too, make sure he wasn't hurt.

Her good feeling didn't last much beyond the opening of the door, though. Colt stood when she entered, dressed in his uniform, his hat in his hands, his bag packed and at his feet.

Sarah knew what she was seeing, and there was nothing left inside for her to say, nothing left for her to do. She stood silent while he explained about leaving, about how he thought it was for the best, even about how he'd come back if he could—but she didn't really hear him. Her heart was breaking too loudly, like a calving glacier, and all the inner sound and turmoil made it impossible to concentrate on his words.

She made herself nod once or twice, giving the illusion of acceptance. That, yes, it was all so reasonable, so understandable. In truth, she didn't understand one damn word he was saying.

Her face hurt with the effort it took to keep her muscles in place. Her brow was furrowed in concentration—she couldn't help that—but the rest of her face was a frozen, blank slate, and it hurt. She'd loved him with everything she had. There was nothing else she could do.

The brass buttons on his double-breasted coat were very bright. She knew she would remember that. And she'd forgotten to ask him how he got his shoes so shiny.

She allowed herself a small sigh for her missed opportunity; it was a release, a safety valve, for the misery welling up inside her.

He reached for her on his way out the door, half a gesture, but she moved aside, shielding herself from his touch with a scant twelve inches of space.

There was nothing else she could do.

Being a responsible person was such hell.

"Ruby? What do you think?" Sarah asked, holding up a beaded sweater.

The flame-haired beautician glanced up from Amanda's dresser drawers. Her prettily plump face was lined with fifty years' worth of Wyoming weather and hard work. She'd been a rancher's wife before she became a beautician.

"Oh yes, my. Peach was such a good color on her. Your dad bought that for her in Reno—Now, honey, don't go—Oh, shoot." She gave up as Sarah dropped the sweater in the church box. "You're probably right. Colt won't be wanting anything Bull bought her, no matter how *expensive*."

Ruby didn't bother to hide her exasperation, and Sarah didn't hide her grin, slight as it was. She'd promised Ruby she'd help, and not even the desertion of a nameless person could make her go back on her word. Though as far as she could tell, doing the right thing or doing the wrong thing didn't make a hill of beans' difference in how her life turned out. It was still empty.

She'd started her period a week ago, and after breaking every damn thing in the Atlas knick-

knack aisle, and causing enough commotion that
Al had come over from the garage to make sure
she was okay . . . Well, after that, she'd made
some decisions.

"What I wouldn't give to be forty pounds lighter,"
Ruby murmured, holding up a pair of brand new
white jeans.

"Cathy Kaye's oldest girl will look great in those.
Why don't you set them aside."

"Seems like we're setting everything aside," Ruby
said, looking around at the separate piles and
boxes of clothes filling the trailer's main bedroom.

"Amanda had a lot of nice things."

"She was a good woman, such a good friend."

Sarah heard the underlying sniffle and braced
herself for another sad interlude. The afternoon
had been full of them. She and Ruby were both
miserable, and truth be known, Sarah was starting to agree with a nameless person. Nobody
needed the closets, so why *did* they have to be out
there at the trailer, wasting an otherwise bearable
day?

She turned back to the shoe boxes in the bottom
of the closet, opening one after the other and
almost automatically stacking them in one of the
larger boxes destined for the church clothing
bank. The last box felt light, and she suspected it
held another pair of sandals. She opened it anyway—she didn't want to be giving away sandals
and find out somebody had received photographs
or love letters—and was surprised to find the box
stuffed with strips of cloth.

Broad stripes of blue and black were jumbled
together like somebody was making quilt pieces.
She pulled the strips out and realized they were

connected by a few odd seams and that the colors overlapped on the individual pieces. Curious, she spread the material on the bed and found cuffs and a collar. It was a shirt, a badly damaged, vaguely familiar shirt.

She held it up. "Ruby? What's this?"

Ruby reached across the corner of the bed and fingered the material. "Looks like a rag, honey. Maybe she used it to polish her shoes."

There were a lot of brown stains on the fabric, mostly coloring the edges of the strips, but they weren't stiff and greasy-feeling like polish. The shirt had been laundered, and Sarah didn't think anybody laundered their shoe-polish rags.

She set the shirt aside and went back to work, but her gaze kept straying to the bed. After a moment, she leaned over and picked up the shirt again. The collar had almost been torn off, but the tag was intact. It was a man's shirt, much too large for Amanda and much too stylish for her father. It must have been Colt's.

Satisfied at least as to why it seemed familiar, she put it back on the bed.

She'd just finished packing Amanda's blouses when Ruby spoke up.

"Let me see that rag again, will you honey?"

Sarah obliged by pushing the shirt toward Ruby. The older woman picked it up.

"I do remember this," she said, shaking her head and giving out a *tsk tsk*. "Amanda was so mad. She bought this shirt for Colt's twentieth birthday. She'd spent more than she really had, but the boy wanted it, and you know how mothers are. Then the next thing you know, the shirt shows up in our Dumpster out behind the shop.

That was when Colt left for his uncle's out in California. You remember, Sarah. You were dating him that summer."

Sarah shifted on the floor, suddenly feeling uncomfortable. No wonder the shreds of material had looked so familiar. She remembered Colt's twentieth birthday, and the shirt, and the whole damn summer that had followed. Those months after he'd left had been the worst time of her life, barring the present, and she didn't want to drag it all out again now. She didn't need or want ten-year-old memories of Colton Haines and his birthday shirt.

"Colt just left," Ruby continued, dropping the shirt on the bed. "You must remember that. Didn't even say good-bye to his own mother."

Damn shirt, Sarah thought, staring at it. Colt had worn it practically every day for two solid weeks after his birthday.

". . . getting tangled up in barbed wire, and then after Amanda realized Colt wasn't coming back, it didn't seem so important. About the shirt, I mean."

"What?" Sarah asked, her head snapping up. "What did you say?"

"Daniel, honey," Ruby repeated. "Daniel Calhoun was the one who told Amanda the story about him and Colt getting drunk and then getting tangled up in the barbed wire. The shirt was such a mess when we found it, all torn up and bloody."

Sarah looked at the shirt again, and with a frightening swiftness put together an unimaginable sequence of events. Just as swiftly she dismissed it all as impossible, because the thoughts trying to form in her mind *were* impossible.

"Funny, isn't it?" Ruby rattled on. "What a mother will keep."

Chiding herself for her unease, Sarah leaned over the bed and picked up the shirt. Her father was a bully, not a sadist. The strips of material slid down her fingers, making them tremble. Colt's blood had stained the frayed edges of the fabric. He'd been wearing the shirt the day they'd made love by the river. She was sure of it. He could have gotten drunk and tangled up in barbed wire, but she'd never seen barbed wire shred a shirt from top to bottom. No, the damage looked like it had been caused by something else.

A sick feeling started in the pit of her stomach. Her father liked intimidation. He liked snapping his whip at stray cats, nervous chickens, and tin cans. But Colt had scars on his body, long marks crossing him front to back. Her father had hit her mother, sometimes more than once, especially when he was in a beating mood, or when a bar fight went bad. He didn't like losing.

Ruby kept talking, mentioning a present she'd bought for one of her boys one time, and how he hadn't taken care of it, either.

Sarah spread the shirt out, quickly, but taking care to lay every strip in place and to keep the back separate from the front. She knew what she was looking for; she remembered how tightly the shirt had fit him. She remembered the beautiful body of the boy she'd loved and of the man she would never stop loving. How his skin was California tan, silky and golden, except for the scars on his chest and back.

When the shirt was arranged, she traced the slash marks with her fingers, seeing exactly which enemy had taken him by surprise and hurt him so badly, and why. Rage and disbelief built to unbearable degrees inside her as her hand slipped down the worn fabric, following her memories of Colt's torso. It was impossible. No man would do that to another.

She remembered then Colt's second leaving, what she'd seen and heard in the parking lot of the Sagebrush. The hatred between the two men had been tangible, a living presence. And suddenly she knew it was true: Her father had whipped Colt that night so long ago, whipped him and left him for his friend to find, a friend who would lie for Colt and never tell. Not even the boy's mother would know.

A drop of moisture hit her hand, then another. She wiped at her cheeks, smearing the angry tears with her fist. She didn't want to believe anything as horrible as the truth in her hands.

"Honey, are you okay?" Ruby asked, but Sarah couldn't answer.

How did Bull live with himself, knowing what he'd done? And how could she live with him? Rock Creek was too small to pretend he didn't exist. How would she get through the days without seeing him and wanting to hurt him as badly as he'd hurt Colt?

She slowly drew the shirt toward her and buried her face in the bold stripes and frayed edges. How would she ever stop crying for Colton Haines?

Twelve

Colt walked across the front porch of Sarah's house, going from window to window and looking inside. All he saw was a whole lot of empty space. There wasn't any soft whiteness at her windows. The flowered curtains in her bedroom were gone. There was nothing left of her washer and dryer in the laundry room off the kitchen except a faucet and a 220 plug. There wasn't any furniture.

He knew what it meant. He'd had his first suspicion when he'd stopped at Atlas Drugs and seen the "Closed" sign out in the middle of the morning.

The rest of the town was bustling. He'd walked through an employment line outside a building that had been empty earlier in the spring. People were lining up for jobs at the big feedlot coming to Rock Creek. The going joke was that the feedlot should find plenty of skilled labor, since there wasn't a man or woman in the whole town who didn't know how to shovel muck. Maybe someday, they said, they'd even get their own packing plant. Suddenly nothing was impossible. Word had it they were even going to elect the new mayor, Peter Barton, king of the whole damn county. So far, he'd done a fine job of developing Rock Creek's potential.

But Atlas Drugs was closed and Sarah's house was empty. Colt ran a hand through his hair and stared out at the Great Plains. The land was parched to the horizon. The spring wildflowers had come and gone, leaving the prairie to grass and the rare blossom. After a good, wet start, the season had gone bone dry. Summer was moving over southeastern Wyoming with heat and sunlight so bright it hurt to look out at the country too long.

He turned back to the house for one last glance, then stepped off the porch and headed for his truck. Ruby would know where she'd gone.

Sarah jammed her feet into her boots and grabbed her jacket with her free hand. Rodeos always started with the bareback-bronc riding, and if she didn't get a move on, she would miss Hank's ride. The Laramie River Rodeo had been his first big win, and he made a point of coming back at least once every year. He was expecting his good-luck charm to be stomping in the stands, cheering him on. The man was in the money, ranked seventh in the world and heading for the jackpot in Las Vegas, the National Finals, with prize money over two million dollars and growing every year.

She checked her purse to make sure she had money to eat. That was city life; a person had to be prepared. In Rock Creek she had run a tab at the cafe. Karla had always known she was good for it. Or most often, she would take money out of her own till and put in an IOU. There had been days when all she'd had in the drawer were her own IOUs.

Now she got a paycheck, a real paycheck, and she liked it. Working as a pharmacist for a grocery store chain had a lot of benefits, like health insurance, paid vacations, sick days, business days, personal days. The list was endless in comparison to her years as one of the struggling self-employed. But the fast-food hamburger stands in Laramie didn't take IOU's, and neither did the concession out at the rodeo arena.

She had twenty dollars, plenty of money to buy herself a hamburger and Hank a beer, if he hung around long enough to drink one. The higher he'd gone in the standings, the more serious he'd become. Last year's world champion bareback rider was only four hundred dollars ahead of him. In professional rodeo, the rankings all came down to money, and the top fifteen money winners in each event went to the National Finals in December.

Hank was determined to get there. Some weekends he barely got off one bronc before he was heading down the road to get on another. He'd had eight years of being wild, and at twenty-six he'd decided it wasn't too late to change, to bear down and claim a place for himself in the record books. The cowboy had a lot of try, and Sarah was pulling for him.

She got almost to the door, when she remembered her earrings. With a groan of pure frustration, she ran back to her bedroom to get her "good luck" earrings. Hank had given them to her as a housewarming present when she'd first moved to Laramie at the end of May. He hadn't had time to deliver them personally, so he'd mailed them. She wanted to show her appreciation by wearing them, and also to share their luck.

Juggling her purse and her jacket, she held the little gold bears to her ears and tried to get the posts in. They weren't teddy bears, but full-grown grizzly bears, done by a goldsmith up in South Dakota, according to Hank's note. They were beautiful, fourteen karat, and made her feel special.

When her doorbell rang, she couldn't believe her luck, or her lack of it. Whoever it was could talk to her on her way to her car. She was out of time.

She finished with her earrings and shrugged into her jacket on her way across the living room. The doorbell rang again, and she muttered that she was coming. She swung the door open with an apology ready on her lips, but it died there unspoken. Apologizing to Colton Haines for anything was taking charity too far. Besides, she'd suddenly lost her voice.

"Looks like I caught you at a bad time," he said after a long moment of silence.

Yes, he had, but she couldn't imagine when a good time might have been for him to walk back into her life. He'd left her again when he shouldn't have, and even though he'd said good-bye, even though he'd had his reasons, she hadn't forgiven him.

"I ought to shoot you." Her voice came back in a

rush of words she wouldn't have consciously chosen. Still, she didn't withdraw them. They were valid enough.

"Whatever it takes." He stood there in his boots and his jeans and his white shirt, looking steady and strong, and ready to take whatever she might give out, good or bad.

"I—I have to get out to the fairgrounds before seven o'clock."

"Can I take you?"

At least he'd asked. "Sure." She couldn't have driven herself anywhere, except into a ditch. She was going a hundred miles an hour inside, her nerves and her pulse in a dead heat for a world speed record. Damn him, sneaking up on her like that. Didn't sailors know how to use a telephone? And what about his writing hand? Had it been broken for two damn months?

In the parking lot, he motioned her toward a metallic-blue king cab pickup truck, a new model with four-wheel drive and California plates. When they were both sitting inside, he started the engine and let it idle for a moment, turning toward her.

"Sarah, I—"

"Nice truck," she interrupted. "King cab. You must do a lot of double-dating."

"No," he said, drawing the word out. "Other than you, I can't even remember the last date I had, let alone the last double date."

"Oh, were we dating?" She gave him a wide-eyed look of innocence. "Is that what you call it?"

She saw his mouth tighten. He turned back to the steering wheel and put the truck in gear. "You know, Sarah, I've always liked that little bitchy streak in you. It keeps me from getting away with murder, lets me know who's really in charge."

She couldn't swear to it, but she thought she saw his mouth twitch, as if the reason he'd tightened it was to keep from grinning at her.

"Bastard."

"I knew this wasn't going to be easy."

And it wasn't. Colt had been cold-shouldered by women before, but nothing like the polar cap Sarah was showing him. At the fairgrounds she told him he didn't have to wait, she'd be able to find her own ride home. He parked anyway and followed her through the haphazard lines of pickup trucks and horse trailers. She was heading toward the bucking chutes and, undoubtably, Hank Cavanaugh—or worse, some other cowboy.

It turned out to be Hank, but Colt couldn't decide whether to be relieved or not. The bronc rider had drawn a wild horse with a bad reputation. Nothing could have made him happier— except having his good-luck charm show up.

He swung Sarah up in his arms with a whoop and a holler. The cowboy was psyched, and Colt couldn't help but grin, even when Hank laid a big kiss on her. He'd thought about Hank while he'd been back in California, telling himself there was no way Sarah would get serious with a cowboy who couldn't stay put.

"Hey, Colton," Hank said over Sarah's shoulder, still holding on to her. "See you made it back all right."

"Still in one piece," Colt replied.

Hank whispered something in her ear, and Sarah nodded. Somehow Colt found that harder to take than the kiss, harder to take than Hank's gloved riding hand slipping down to pat her bottom a few times.

"For luck," the cowboy said, grinning at him.

"You might need more than you think," he answered. He hated sounding like a macho jerk, but things between him and Sarah were too unsettled for him to be casual.

Hank just grinned and winked, then gave her one more hug before heading back to where the other riders were stretching out and getting ready behind the chutes.

Colt tried to pay for her soda and nachos at the concession stand, but she refused his offer. She did find a place in the stands where he was able to sit beside her, which he took as an encouraging step in the right direction. She wouldn't look at him, though, and every time they accidentally brushed up against each other, she flinched.

He couldn't recall a small action ever bothering him so much. Every time she pulled away, it hurt him. She hadn't flinched when Hank had touched her; she'd held on to him like he was a lifeline. Like Cavanaugh was somebody she could count on not to let her down, not to leave her.

The announcer's voice broke into his thoughts and captured his attention with the name on his mind.

"Let's hear it for Hank Cavanaugh, folks. A top cowboy from Huron, South Dakota, in chute number two, riding Warpaint, a bronc who hasn't been ridden in his last ten times out. But we've got a cowboy in there getting ready to show old Warpaint how it's done. Come on, Hank. It's only eight seconds' worth of trouble."

The chute flew open at Hank's nod, and Warpaint came out bucking a blaze of fury. The cowboy's spurs marked him high, and Sarah came to her feet.

"Come on, Hank. *Ride him*," she whispered, her gaze trained on the spectacle of man against beast.

Colt looked up at her, and for the first time it hit him just exactly what he'd walked away from two months ago, and just exactly what it was that had made him come back. Watching her pull for her friend made him realize why he'd needed her when no one else would do. It wasn't an indefinable love, and it was more than what he felt when they made love.

The wind caught her hair, lifting and floating the strands in gossamer trails against a blue evening sky. She turned, following the action in the arena, and sunlight caught the delicate profile of her face. She was beautiful and constant, someone to believe in, someone to count on. She knew what she valued and she took good care of those she loved—when they let her.

For a while, at different times and in different ways, he'd been part of what she valued, someone she'd loved, and those had been his finest moments.

A brief, ironic smile curved his mouth. He'd been trained to conquer, and he'd come back to the woman who left him feeling helpless. She took no prisoners. It was surrender, total and complete.

The rest of the crowd was on their feet, cheering crazily as Hank grabbed on to the pickup man whose job it was to get the cowboys off the bucking horses. He left Warpaint ridden hard and for the money. Colt watched as Hank picked his hat up out of the dirt and waved to the fans, and he added his applause to everybody else's, rising to stand next to Sarah.

She looked at him then, willingly, and he smiled at her. He knew she was justified in keeping him at a distance. He'd screwed up, and she was going to have him on his knees before the night was over. He might as well prepare himself.

They watched the rest of the bareback riders, with Sarah keeping track of the scores to make sure Hank won with his phenomenal eighty-four point ride. He did.

"Well, that's it," she said when the last score was announced.

"I thought he rode saddle-broncs."

"He used to," she said, gathering up her nachos and purse. "But he's started specializing, putting all his money and energy into bareback riding."

"Are you going over to say good-bye?" Colt thought he might skip that part.

She shook her head. "He's got a morning slack in Cheyenne tomorrow. He's probably already left. He said he'd rather get there and sleep than have to drive early in the morning."

Colt couldn't fault his reasoning, yet he couldn't help but wonder if his presence had helped decide Hank's schedule. For the kind of miles a rodeo cowboy put on, getting from Laramie to Cheyenne was a walk in the park.

"Can I take you out to dinner? For a steak somewhere?" he asked. It was a straight question. He meant nothing by it except that he wanted to sit someplace and share a meal with the woman he had never been able to forget.

She looked away, then back toward the arena, and for an awful moment he thought she was going to turn him down, tell him to get lost and never come around again.

She did.

"No. No, I don't think so," she said, still looking out at the arena, where the steer-wrestling was getting ready to start. As if guilt had gotten the better of her, she gave him a brief glance. "I don't mean anything by it, Colt, really I don't. You're— you're the best. I mean that. I just don't want to go with you. Thanks for the ride."

And with that, she was gone.

He didn't believe it. It was impossible. There was no reason for her to leave him like that, standing in the bleachers with his heart and his pride slipping down around his ankles. She had every right to be angry, but they were supposed to talk things out, work things out. She wasn't supposed to walk away from him.

But she was walking all right, and she already had a good ten yards on him.

He swore, one succinct word that got him a few sidelong glances, and took out after her.

He lost her once in the maze of trucks and trailers, and he knew a moment of true panic, the kind where a man's heart lodges in his throat with the force of a piston thrust. Then he caught sight of blond hair. He skirted around a group of kids heading toward the concession stand and got tripped up on a particularly little one, tangling himself with about thirty-five pounds of pure tough.

"Hey, mister." A bony elbow jabbed him in the knee. "Get off me."

Colt was trying to get out from around the boy, who from Colt's point of view looked like nothing more than a hand-me-down cowboy hat and a pair of baggy Wranglers. They sidestepped each other in the wrong direction twice, and the boy kicked him with his small pointy-toed boot. Then he burst into tears and yelled for his sister.

"Annn-nnieee!"

Colt grabbed his shin and looked up in time to get the threatening look that big sister Annie gave him. She whisked the little boy off his feet and swung him onto her hip. The whole incident took about thirty seconds—long enough for Sarah to disappear.

He took out after her again, limping the first couple of steps. Things weren't going right. They weren't going right at all.

He caught up with her at the fence. He reached for her, thought better of it, and with effort got ahead of her.

"Sarah." He took a couple of steps backward as he faced her, expecting her to stop. Thankfully, she did. "Sarah. We need to talk."

"Talk?" She looked surprised.

"Yes. I've got some things I have to say. Some things I need to explain . . . about why I left, and I—"

"No. You don't need to explain anything." Her gaze faltered. "You were right, Colt. We hurt each other too much. I'm even more guilty than you are. You don't need to apologize. You don't owe me explanations."

Sarah? Hurt him? He was momentarily speechless. When she started to move away, though, he found his voice in a hurry.

"You have never hurt me." She kept walking, and this time he did reach for her, holding her gently around her arm with his hand. "Missing you has hurt me, remembering you has hurt, but you have always been kind and loving, sweet and generous, giving me more than any person has a right to expect, and all I'm asking for is a chance."

"A chance for what?" She looked up, her eyes filled with a guilt he didn't understand. "A chance for some other bastard to come along and strip the skin off your back? All because you loved me? Was it worth it, Colt?" Her voice broke. "Was it worth it?"

"Yes." His answer was as clear and steady as his gaze, which held hers. "I made you mine that first night, and it gave me a reason to believe I could make you mine again. I'm here because I love you, Sarah."

She was quiet for a long moment, shifting her gaze from his face to the toes of her boots. "He's lucky you didn't kill him. I almost did myself."

"Did Daniel tell you?"

"No. Ruby and I found the shirt in your mom's closet. It took me a while, but I finally figured out what must have happened, and when. God, I'm sorry, Colt. I knew he was a son of a bitch, but I never dreamed he'd do anything like that. I swear. I never would have left, if I'd known. Toby or no Toby."

Colt took her nachos and set them on the hood of the nearest truck. "You weren't going to eat those, were you?"

"No."

He held her hand, caressing it with his thumb. "I was going to tell you myself, later tonight, but what I was trying to explain just now was why I left you at your house in April, not why I left ten years ago."

"I think I already know that too," she said, carefully holding herself apart from him.

He laughed quietly. "Yeah. I guess if you thought about killing him yourself, you probably understand. It's a scary thing, hating somebody, but it's not near as complicated as loving somebody, especially in the long run."

With an easy tug, she pulled her hand free. "What do you want, Colt?" Though she wouldn't look at him, the words came out more challenge than question, like she was expecting the worst and the least of him.

He was glad that this time he could prove her wrong. "I want you. I want us together. I want to sell my land in Rock Creek and make a new start, maybe right here in Albany County. I'd like to try my hand at ranching again, and see if I'd make a good math teacher somewhere. I want kids of my own, and I want you to be their mom. I've been thinking that you might have wanted to pick out your own wedding rings, but that it would be better if I came with something I could put on your finger in case I got lucky and you said yes."

"You want a lot," she said, crossing her arms over her chest.

"I'm a selfish bastard," he agreed. Her nod surprised him nonetheless, compelling him to add points in his own defense. "I still have to resign my commission, but after that I'll never leave you. I've got two weeks, and I want to be married before then. We can still have all the good years together." He leaned his head to one side to look at her face. "Sarah? What do you think?" God, it had taken a lot of guts to ask that, just as it now took a lot of patience to wait for her answer.

He waited as she scuffed a mark in the dirt with the toe of her boot. He waited through a sigh that sounded heavy with indecision, and then he waited some more.

Finally she spoke.

"I think I'd like to hear the part again about why you're here." She looked up at him through her lashes, and he thought he detected the slightest smile on her mouth.

"That little part?" he asked. "You want to hear that little part again?"

"Yes."

"Okay." He reached for her hand, glancing around as he pulled her into the shadows provided by the setting sun and the horse trailer they were standing next to.

When he had her situated where he wanted her, close enough to feel her breathe, her hands against his chest and the rest of her just simply and seriously pressed against him; when he had one hand caressing her waist and the other sliding through her hair; when he had her remembering how good love could be with the man who loved her, he bent his head and whispered in her ear.

"I'm here because of everything you are, everything you've ever been to me. You're the most beautiful woman I've ever known. Every time I see you, something happens inside me, and I need that something like I need air. You're the best part of me, Sarah, and I want to be the best part of you."

He felt her hands slide over his shoulders and

meet behind his neck, and he kissed her, a light brushing of his mouth over the velvet softness of her cheek.

"I love you, Colton Haines." Her voice was a whisper, and her arms tightened around him. "I love you."

He wasn't going to ask for more, but she turned toward him and their lips met. He instinctively pulled her closer. He wanted her; he never seemed to stop wanting her. He held his breath and felt the heat rising, drifting up his body, and he lowered his mouth to hers.

Sarah felt the vibrations of his groan echo in her mouth, setting off a chain reaction of impulses. He was gentle and seductive, his tongue slipping inside to taste and tease, until with the subtlest of reactions she signaled her acquiescence. He asked for more then, and took everything she gave.

She'd been so afraid of loving him, even of being with him. She'd mentally kicked herself a hundred times on the way to the rodeo for letting him drive her to the fairgrounds, for thinking she could simply accept a friendly gesture and not want more. Turning down his offer of dinner had been her one intelligent decision where he was concerned, and she'd applauded her good sense all the way across the lot. It had helped her hold back the tears she was so damn tired of crying for him.

But he'd surprised her, not with his love, but with his telling her about it. If they hadn't somehow gotten started kissing, she was sure he'd still be telling her how he felt. Not that she was complaining. She was going to give him a lifetime of chances to say *I love you, Sarah. . . . I'm here because I love you.*

Colt slipped his hands down over her hips and cupped her buttocks, caressing the slope from her waist to her thighs, feeling the firm, erotic curves. It was almost too much, yet it wasn't nearly enough. He moved his hands to a place that didn't give him such crazy ideas and broke off the kiss. It was survival time.

"This means yes, right?"

"Yes?" she asked, wonderfully breathless.

"You'll marry me." He gave it to her as a statement of fact, but was still gratified to hear her answer.

"Yes."

"And I can take you home?" He wasn't taking anything for granted.

"Yes."

"And I can stay with you there, tonight?" He was taking absolutely nothing for granted. "It's been a long two months. I would have written, but I was on a submarine most of the time, and my love life is not considered priority mail."

He kissed her again, just because she was there and her mouth was so damn sweet, better than honey. He kissed her until he had to stop, but he couldn't stop the feelings and the memories. He didn't want to stop them. He wanted her to know what she did to him, how beautiful she was.

"All I thought about was you. I tried every distraction known to man, and still, when I went to bed at night, all I could think about was how soft you are inside, and how you taste, all over, and the way you—"

"Yes," he heard her whisper, just before she pulled his mouth back down on hers.

He loved how she said yes. She had a thousand ways of saying yes, and he loved every one of them.

THE EDITOR'S CORNER

Soon we'll be rushing into the holiday season, and we have some special LOVESWEPT books to bring you good cheer. Nothing can put you in a merrier mood than the six fabulous romances coming your way next month.

The first book in our lineup is **PRIVATE LESSONS** by Barbara Boswell, LOVESWEPT #582. Biology teacher Gray McCall remembers the high school student who'd had a crush on him, but now Elissa Emory is all grown up and quite a knockout. Since losing his family years ago, he hadn't teased or flirted with a woman, but he can't resist when Elissa challenges him to a sizzling duel of heated embraces and fiery kisses. Extracurricular activity has never been as tempting as it is in Barbara's vibrantly written romance.

With **THE EDGE OF PARADISE,** LOVESWEPT #583, Peggy Webb will tug at your heartstrings—and her hero will capture your heart. David Kelly is a loner, a man on the run who's come looking for sanctuary in a quiet Southern town. Still, he can't hide his curiosity—or yearning—for the lovely woman who lives next door. When he feels the ecstasy of being in Rosalie Brown's arms, he begins to wonder if he has left trouble behind and finally found paradise. A superb love story from Peggy!

Only Jan Hudson can come up with a heroine whose ability to accurately predict the weather stems from her once having been struck by lightning! And you can read all about it in **SUNNY SAYS,** LOVESWEPT #584. Kale Hoaglin is skeptical of Sunny Larkin's talent, and that's a problem since he's the new owner of the small TV station where Sunny works as the weather reporter. But her unerring predictions—and thrilling kisses—soon make a believer of him. Jan continues to delight with her special blend of love and laughter.

Please give a rousing welcome to new author Deborah Harmse and her first novel, **A MAN TO BELIEVE IN**, LOVESWEPT #585. This terrific story begins when Cori McLaughlin attends a costume party and catches the eye of a wickedly good-looking pirate. Jake Tanner can mesmerize any woman, and Cori's determined not to fall under his spell. But to be the man in her life, Jake is ready to woo her with patience, persistence, and passion. Enjoy one of our New Faces of 1992!

Michael Knight feels as if he's been **STRUCK BY LIGHTNING** when he first sees Cassidy Harrold, in LOVESWEPT #586 by Patt Bucheister. A mysterious plot of his matchmaking father brought him to England, and with one glimpse of Cassidy, he knows he'll be staying around for a while. Cassidy has always had a secret yen for handsome cowboys, and tangling with the ex–rodeo star is wildly exciting, but can she be reckless enough to leave London behind for his Montana home? Don't miss this enthralling story from Patt!

Tonya Wood returns to LOVESWEPT with **SNEAK**, #587, and this wonderful romance has definitely been worth waiting for. When Nicki Sharman attacks the intruder in her apartment, she thinks he's an infamous cat burglar. But he turns out to be Val Santisi, the rowdy bad boy she's adored since childhood. He's working undercover to chase a jewel thief, and together they solve the mystery of who's robbing the rich—and steal each other's heart in the process. Welcome back, Tonya!

FANFARE presents four spectacular novels that are on sale this month. Ciji Ware, the acclaimed author of *Romantic Times* award-winner **ISLAND OF THE SWANS**, delivers

WICKED COMPANY, an engrossing love story set in London during the eighteenth century. As Sophie Mc-Gann moves through the fascinating—and bawdy—world of Drury Lane, she remains loyal to her dream . . . and the only man she has ever loved.

Trouble runs deep in **STILL WATERS,** a novel of gripping suspense and sensual romance by Tami Hoag, highly praised author of **LUCKY'S LADY.** When the body of a murder victim literally falls at Elizabeth Stuart's feet, she's branded a suspect. But Sheriff Dane Jantzen soon becomes convinced of her innocence, and together they must find the killer before another deadly strike can cost them their chance for love, even her very life.

In the grand tradition of **THORN BIRDS** comes **THE DREAMTIME LEGACY** by Norma Martyn, an epic novel of Australia and one unforgettable woman. Jenny Garnett is indomitable as she travels through life, from a childhood in a penal colony to her marriage to a mysterious aristocrat, from the harshness of aching poverty to the splendor of unthinkable riches.

Treat yourself to **MORE THAN FRIENDS,** the classic romance by bestselling author BJ James. In this charming novel, corporate magnate John Michael Bradford meets his match when he's rescued from a freak accident by diminutive beauty Jamie Brent. Mike always gets what he wants, and what he wants is Jamie. But growing up with six brothers has taught independent Jamie never to surrender to a man who insists on always being in control.

Also on sale this month in the hardcover edition from Doubleday is **LAST SUMMER** by Theresa Weir. The author of **FOREVER** has penned yet another passionate and emotionally moving tale, one that brings together a bad-boy actor and the beautiful widow who tames his heart.

The Delaneys are coming next month from FANFARE! This legendary family's saga continues with **THE DELANEY CHRISTMAS CAROL,** three original and sparkling novellas by none other than Iris Johansen, Kay Hooper, and Fayrene Preston. Read about three generations of Delaneys in love and the changing faces of Christmas past, present, and future—only from FANFARE.

Happy reading!

With best wishes,

Nita Taublib

Nita Taublib
Associate Publisher
LOVESWEPT and FANFARE

OFFICIAL RULES TO WINNERS CLASSIC SWEEPSTAKES

No Purchase necessary. To enter the sweepstakes follow instructions found elsewhere in this offer. You can also enter the sweepstakes by hand printing your name, address, city, state and zip code on a 3" x 5" piece of paper and mailing it to: Winners Classic Sweepstakes, P.O. Box 785, Gibbstown, NJ 08027. Mail each entry separately. Sweepstakes begins 12/1/91. Entries must be received by 6/1/93. Some presentations of this sweepstakes may feature a deadline for the Early Bird prize. If the offer you receive does, then to be eligible for the Early Bird prize your entry must be received according to the Early Bird date specified. Not responsible for lost, late, damaged, misdirected, illegible or postage due mail. Mechanically reproduced entries are not eligible. All entries become property of the sponsor and will not be returned.

Prize Selection/Validations: Winners will be selected in random drawings on or about 7/30/93, by VENTURA ASSOCIATES, INC., an independent judging organization whose decisions are final. Odds of winning are determined by total number of entries received. Circulation of this sweepstakes is estimated not to exceed 200 million. Entrants need not be present to win. All prizes are guaranteed to be awarded and delivered to winners. Winners will be notified by mail and may be required to complete an affidavit of eligibility and release of liability which must be returned within 14 days of date of notification or alternate winners will be selected. Any guest of a trip winner will also be required to execute a release of liability. Any prize notification letter or any prize returned to a participating sponsor, Bantam Doubleday Dell Publishing Group, Inc., its participating divisions or subsidiaries, or VENTURA ASSOCIATES, INC. as undeliverable will be awarded to an alternate winner. Prizes are not transferable. No multiple prize winners except as may be necessary due to unavailability, in which case a prize of equal or greater value will be awarded. Prizes will be awarded approximately 90 days after the drawing. All taxes, automobile license and registration fees, if applicable, are the sole responsibility of the winners. Entry constitutes permission (except where prohibited) to use winners' names and likenesses for publicity purposes without further or other compensation.

Participation: This sweepstakes is open to residents of the United States and Canada, except for the province of Quebec. This sweepstakes is sponsored by Bantam Doubleday Dell Publishing Group, Inc. (BDD), 666 Fifth Avenue, New York, NY 10103. Versions of this sweepstakes with different graphics will be offered in conjunction with various solicitations or promotions by different subsidiaries and divisions of BDD. Employees and their families of BDD, its division, subsidiaries, advertising agencies, and VENTURA ASSOCIATES, INC., are not eligible.

Canadian residents, in order to win, must first correctly answer a time limited arithmetical skill testing question. Void in Quebec and wherever prohibited or restricted by law. Subject to all federal, state, local and provincial laws and regulations.

Prizes: The following values for prizes are determined by the manufacturers' suggested retail prices or by what these items are currently known to be selling for at the time this offer was published. Approximate retail values include handling and delivery of prizes. Estimated maximum retail value of prizes: 1 Grand Prize ($27,500 if merchandise or $25,000 Cash); 1 First Prize ($3,000); 5 Second Prizes ($400 each); 35 Third Prizes ($100 each); 1,000 Fourth Prizes ($9.00 each) ; 1 Early Bird Prize ($5,000); Total approximate maximum retail value is $50,000. Winners will have the option of selecting any prize offered at level won. Automobile winner must have a valid driver's license at the time the car is awarded. Trips are subject to space and departure availability. Certain black-out dates may apply. Travel must be completed within one year from the time the prize is awarded. Minors must be accompanied by an adult. Prizes won by minors will be awarded in the name of parent or legal guardian.

For a list of Major Prize Winners (available after 7/30/93): send a self-addressed, stamped envelope entirely separate from your entry to: Winners Classic Sweepstakes Winners, P.O. Box 825, Gibbstown, NJ 08027. Requests must be received by 6/1/93. DO NOT SEND ANY OTHER CORRESPONDENCE TO THIS P.O. BOX.

The Delaney Dynasty lives on in

The Delaney Christmas Carol

by Kay Hooper, Iris Johansen, & Fayrene Preston

Three of romantic fiction's best-loved authors present the changing face of Christmas spirit—past, present, and future—as they tell the story of three generations of Delaneys in love.

CHRISTMAS PAST by Iris Johansen

From the moment he first laid eyes on her, Kevin Delaney felt a curious attraction for the ragclad Gypsy beauty rummaging through the attic of his ranch at Killara. He didn't believe for a moment her talk of magic mirrors and second-sight, but something about Zara St. Cloud stirred his blood. Now, as Christmas draws near, a touch leads to a kiss and a gift of burning passion.

CHRISTMAS PRESENT by Fayrene Preston

Bria Delaney had been looking for Christmas ornaments in her mother's attic, when she saw him in the mirror for the first time—a stunningly handsome man with sky-blue eyes and red-gold hair. She had almost convinced herself he was only a dream when Kells Braxton arrived at Killara and led them both to a holiday wonderland of sensuous pleasure.

CHRISTMAS FUTURE by Kay Hooper

As the last of the Delaney men, Brett returned to Killara this Christmastime only to find it in the capable hands of his father's young and beautiful widow. Yet the closer he got to Cassie, the more Brett realized that the embers of their old love still burned and that all it would take was a look, a kiss, a caress, to turn their dormant passion into an inferno.

The best in Women's Fiction from Bantam FANFARE.
On sale in November 1992   AN 428 9/92